The gate slammed open. "Go! Go! Go!" Hannah yelled.

Ebony's power came alive. He shot toward the first barrel, neck forward. Ebony leaned to the right into the first corner, thrusting his front hooves to the left of his body, driving himself around the barrel. *Don't slip, Ebony.* They took the corner tight, in control.

*Now, Ebony, now! Rocket us out of here!...*

"Hustle now! Hustle in between!" Hannah had heard Uncle Joe say many times. She focused her attention on the third barrel, anticipating Ebony's deep lean to the left. She guided Ebony's approach, careful not to overshoot it, to use the speed they built to drive them around it. Power under control, power focused on that loop around the barrel, that kind of power took Hannah's breath away.

Other books in the
# Hannah's
*Island*
## S E R I E S

A Hound for Hannah
The Mystery of the Sunken Steamboat
The Mysterious Stranger
The Lesson of the Ancient Bones
The Secret of the Old Well
The Texas Rodeo Showdown

## *About the Author*

Eric E. Wiggin was born on a farm in Albion, Maine, in 1939. As a former Maine pastor, Yankee school–teacher, news reporter, and editor of a Maine–published Christian newspaper, Wiggin is intimately familiar with the Pine Tree State and her people. He has strived to model Hannah and Walt after courageous examples of the Maine Christian youth he knows well.

Wiggin's ancestors include Hannah Bradstreet Wiggin, and one of his four granddaughters is Hannah Snyder. But his greatest model for the *Hannah's Island* series is Hannah, mother of the prophet Samuel, known for her faith and courage in adversity.

Wiggin's thirteen novels for youth and adults are set in rural or small-town Maine. The woods, fields, and pasture lanes of the Wiggin family farm sloping toward a vast Waldo County bog furnish a natural tapestry for the setting of many of his books.

Author Wiggin now lives in rural Fruitport, Michigan, with his wife, Dorothy.

# The Texas Rodeo Showdown

## Eric Wiggin

**Emerald Books**

P.O. Box 635
Lynnwood, WA 98046

# Contents

1. Rodeo Dreams . . . . . . . . . . . . . . . . . . . . 7

2. A Wild, Wet Idea . . . . . . . . . . . . . . . . . . 15

3. Only Fantasy? . . . . . . . . . . . . . . . . . . . 21

4. Flying High . . . . . . . . . . . . . . . . . . . . 30

5. Left Out . . . . . . . . . . . . . . . . . . . . . . 41

6. Wrestling the World . . . . . . . . . . . . . . . 50

7. New Boots and a Million Candles . . . . . . 56

8. Runaway . . . . . . . . . . . . . . . . . . . . . . 67

9. "Ride 'em, Cowgirl!" . . . . . . . . . . . . . . . 76

10. Hannah the Spy . . . . . . . . . . . . . . . . . . 87

11. A Crummy Party . . . . . . . . . . . . . . . . . 97

12. The Star of the Pageant . . . . . . . . . . . 107

13. Hamstring Harvey . . . . . . . . . . . . . . . 115

14. Rodeo Danger . . . . . . . . . . . . . . . . . . 123

15. Black Lightning . . . . . . . . . . . . . . . . . 133

16. Stage Fright . . . . . . . . . . . . . . . . . . . 142

17. Barreling Along . . . . . . . . . . . . . . . . . 150

18. Stuck-Up . . . . . . . . . . . . . . . . . . . . . 160

19. The Showdown . . . . . . . . . . . . . . . . . . 168

20. An Old Family Story . . . . . . . . . . . . . . 176

# Chapter One

# Rodeo Dreams

"The Texas Mesquite Rodeo is coming to the state fair?!" Hannah grinned, and her emerald green eyes sparkled. She held up the flyer she'd just dug from a grocery bag as she helped unload their big motor launch after Mama's shopping trip to the mainland. "From Dallas, Texas—all the way to Maine?"

"Looks like it," Mama said, handing Hannah another brown bag. "There are posters up all over Laketon, right next to the signs advertising this fall's Skowhegan State Fair."

"Wow," Hannah whispered. "That's the rodeo I've seen on TV. It'd be fun to ride Ebony in it!" Hannah glanced up the hill to where her brother Walt was riding their black stallion bareback to chase the steer back into the pasture.

Mama stepped from the boat onto the dock. "Uncle Joe has you hooked on rodeo, doesn't he?"

The Parmenters had no TV in their tourist lodge on Beaver Island in vast, blue Moosehead Lake. But Hannah sometimes watched television when she

7

visited Uncle Joe and Aunt Theresa Boudreau in Laketon, on the mainland.

"Yeah," Hannah said. "Uncle Joe loves to watch rodeo on the Nashville Country and Western channel." Hannah slipped the rodeo flyer into the hip pocket of her jeans. She then gave her wagonload of groceries a tug and hurried from the boat dock toward the wide front porch of grand, pine-log Beaver Lodge. Mama followed up the flagstone walk, pushing a big wheelbarrow of groceries. Running a busy island tourist lodge was hard work, but Hannah loved it. She got to share her home with interesting folks from cities all over America.

"Your Uncle Joe does imagine himself quite a cowboy," Mama chuckled. "He was a horse handler for Northwoods Logging, way up in the Allagash Wilderness."

"I *know* that, Mama!" As she and Mama carried the grocery bags up the stairs, Hannah thought about the powerful Percheron and Belgian work-horses Uncle Joe once handled for logging crews. She grinned and shot another glance at Ebony, now munching on grass in the pasture. Once a race-horse, the tall stallion had been Hannah's special steed since Papa had brought him across the ice from the mainland one winter to haul tourists on sleigh rides. "I'm gonna enter me'n Ebony in that rodeo barrel racing contest!" Hannah said. She imagined herself leaning dangerously on Ebony as he slowed from a wild gallop to tightly circle the barrels, lightning fast, without striking a single one. She heard the crowd cheering them on.

"You've got to get Ebony off our island first," Mama murmured. "It's more than a mile to the mainland."

"I know, Mama." Hannah sighed and let the

kitchen screen door shut with a bang. She set the last two grocery bags on the counter. Living on your own island in a lake was fun, but it had its problems. Like getting a horse to the rodeo, for instance.

"R-r-rowff!" Hannah's tricolored basset-Lab hound, Hunter, woke from his nap beside the kitchen's wood-burning range. The clatter of the screen door from the porch had disturbed his midday dream of chasing snowshoe hares out of the garden.

"C'mon, feller!" Hannah knelt and scratched her long-legged, flop-eared pet behind his silky ears. "Let's go for a trot. Can we, Mama?" Whenever she had something important to think about, Hannah liked to ride across their island alone, just she and Ebony and Hunter.

"If Walter's done with the horse. Be back in time to milk Molly. Oh, and you and Walt will have to take care of Papa's barn chores, too. He's down the lake with a boatload of guests. Then he has to meet a couple from New York at the dock in Laketon, you know."

"I wi...yee-ouch!" Hannah extracted her long, strawberry blonde French braid from Hunter's too-friendly teeth, where he had given it a playful tug.

Once outside, Hannah slung her Western saddle across the top rail of the pasture bars and led Ebony to the fence so she could saddle him.

Walt was chasing a steer around the pasture like a crazy man. Hannah stood on the bottom rail of the fence and leaned over into the pasture. "What are you doing?" she yelled. "Trying to get yourself killed?"

Walt grinned. "I'm steer rasslin'! You know, like we've seen on Uncle Joe's rodeo videos. Watch." He chased a young steer from behind until he had a grip on its horns. He struggled to hold its head between his arms against his chest. They skidded back and forth. Walt twisted, but instead of sprawling on its back, the animal went down on its front legs. Walt lost his grip, and the animal scrambled up, then shook his stubby horns and scurried across the hillside pasture with an angry rumble of hooves.

"You...you knew about the big Texas rodeo already and you didn't tell me?"

Walt dusted his clothes off and hoisted himself onto the fence. "I just found out yesterday when I took the boat to Laketon to get the mail. Since there's *no way* you can get Ebony to the mainland until the lake freezes, I didn't want you to feel bad."

"What about you? Aren't you supposed to have a horse?"

"Yeah, I'm supposed to chase the steer out of the chute on horseback, then slide off the horse onto the steer's shoulders and wrestle him down. Right now, I'm just trying to get used to the wrestling part."

"But what about later?" Hannah hoped he wasn't counting on using Ebony, but even if he were, he'd have the same problem she had.

Walt shrugged. "I still have to figure out a way to practice, but for the junior steer wrestling, the rodeo people decided to furnish a horse if you need it—and the steer, of course."

"Oh?" Hannah was quiet for a moment.

"I don't see how you can possibly get Ebony to the rodeo."

"You've got that figured right!" Hannah said. She climbed up on the gate of wooden bars and clapped her big saddle onto Ebony's powerful back while Walt held the horse's bridle.

"Oh," Walt added, "I grabbed an extra application

for the contests. Maybe you can figure something out."

"Fat chance!" It suddenly seemed to Hannah that Walt was teasing her with the extra form. Hadn't he already said that things were hopeless? Hannah yanked Ebony's tether around a gatepost and headed toward the barn, where Papa had installed an extension phone in the cow tie-up. She felt like talking to Caylin. Caylin Coulson had started out as Walt's friend, since they were in the same Sunday school class, but she had become Hannah's best friend, too, even though she was more than a year older.

"Walt *totally* gets the breaks," Hannah said as soon as Caylin answered the phone. "He's entering the Texas Mesquite Rodeo, and can I? No. I can't get my horse to the stupid mainland."

"Slow down," Caylin said softly. "You don't need to shout at *me*."

Hannah paced restlessly around the barn as far as the phone cord let her. "Sorry," she said more quietly. "I just really want to do this."

"I know. I was with Walt yesterday when he got the forms."

"You knew about it already, too?"

"Yeah. He was going to try to figure out how to tell you. He knows you love barrel racing. Says you've read books and watched tons of videos."

"Walt said that?" Hannah kicked at some stray pieces of hay. "I know I need to practice a lot, and I know I might not win if professional riders come, but I really want to try."

"There's *got* to be a way to get Ebony to the mainland, Han. You can do it."

"You think so?" Hannah felt better to have another person believe it could be done.

"You gotta try."

Hannah twisted the spiral phone cord around her finger. "I guess I *could* have entered the Miss Lakeland pageant, like you. But I couldn't see myself in a frilly dress singing for all those people." Hannah thought of pretty, blue-eyed, flame-haired Caylin. Caylin always looked good on stage. Hannah could sing, but singing to entertain a crowd just wasn't Hannah's idea of fun—even if the girl who won the Miss Lakeland contest in Laketon would get to perform at the big pageant the night after the rodeo. Hannah didn't want to sing. She wanted to ride.

"Listen," Caylin said. "I really gotta go, but I promise I'll help you think of a way."

"Think hard. And hey, maybe next time I come to town you can show me what you're going to sing."

"Sure, later. Bye."

"Bye."

Moments later, Hannah tucked the toe of her riding boot into a stirrup and swung into the saddle. "Let's go, guys!" Even though Caylin had been in a hurry, the short conversation with her had made Hannah feel better. Hannah whistled for Hunter, then clucked at Ebony, urging him up the hillside pasture toward the road through the forest.

"We're getting you to the mainland for that rodeo, Ebony," Hannah promised as she guided her tall, black horse along the mossy woods road beneath the tall pines. "I'm not the only one who thinks we can do it."

Hannah even laughed out loud as a bushy-tailed gray squirrel, alarmed at Hunter the hound's intrusion into the sheltering woodland, sent up an angry racket. As Ebony's hooves rattled across the plank bridge where Bog Brook tumbled down Bald Hill into the marsh, the squirrel's chattering was picked up by a blue jay.

"You don't want t' nose around in that old Indian cemetery, boy," Hannah said, half an hour later. They were on the far side of Beaver Island now, and Hunter bounded merrily from the raspberry bushes that overgrew the ancient graveyard. "Hup!" Hannah called to Ebony. She clapped her straw cowgirl hat tighter on her head and flipped her French braid behind her.

The horse took off at a trot, and Hunter loped beside them. Hannah guided her handsome, coal-black steed around a pile of brush left by Papa's loggers. Then she slapped the reins, urging Ebony to run. She leaned across his flowing mane, clutching the stallion's ribs as he cleared a large log in a flying bound.

"Arr-uff!"

Hannah and Ebony shared the hound's surprise. "Whoa, boy!" Hannah reined Ebony in. "Heel! Hist!" she called to Hunter.

A large, long-legged, brown animal, tall as Ebony but skinny, stood up to its belly in a thicket of young firs. The startled creature stared with warm, brown eyes at Hannah, Ebony, and Hunter, and its ears twitched anxiously.

"Cute," Hannah said quietly.

A moose calf slipped from the fir thicket and nuzzled up to the cow moose, its mother.

"A calf!" Hannah watched, breathless.

Another brown baby moose burst from among the firs.

"Wow! Twins!" This time, Hannah spoke aloud in surprise.

"Whff-whff-whff-whff!" Ebony blew through his lips.

"Arf!" Hunter barked.

*I've never known how moose get on our island,* Hannah thought. *Now I guess I'm going to find out.* Mama Moose and her earth-toned twins splashed into the lake, walking toward the distant point of land that reached from the mainland toward the back of Beaver Island.

# A Wild, Wet Idea

Hannah leaned over the horn of her Western saddle. She pulled down the brim of her hat and squinted across the glistening water, watching the three moose and thinking. Talking with Caylin had helped. But Hannah had to admit that during the entire ride across the island, she hadn't thought of one good idea about how to get Ebony to the mainland. She knew well enough that the only boat around Laketon that could haul a grown horse was an old logging tugboat that hadn't been used in years. What other way was there?

*Isn't there some way, God? Some way to get Ebony off this island?*

Hannah pulled the flyer from her pocket. The contest had divisions for teens thirteen and up—and Hannah would be thirteen just before the fair opened. Hannah felt her disappointment rise again, and she crammed the flyer back into her pocket. It made her just a teensy bit mad to think about Walt practicing for the steer-wrestling contest.

*I can ride about as good as any kid in this*

*county,* Hannah thought. She sighed in frustration. No matter how good her riding skills were, she might not get to compete. There'd be kids from all over Maine in the contests. *Maybe I should have entered the Miss Lakeland pageant in Laketon like Caylin,* she told herself. But it was too late. The deadline had passed, and now Hannah would be shut out of both contests.

Hannah watched the mother moose and calves splash along, hurried on their way by Hunter, who barked as they raced towards the opposite shore. The cow moose was far offshore now, still wading in the shallow water along a submerged sandbar. The moose calves, with shorter legs, were already swimming.

"Cool!" Hannah laughed aloud as Mama Moose splashed behind each calf, nudging her babies with her long snout. An idea began to form in Hannah's mind as to how she might get Ebony to the mainland for the riding contest.

"Oh!" Hannah squealed, as the big female cow moose suddenly disappeared completely into deep water beyond the underwater sandbar. "Ah-hh!" Hannah sighed in relief as Mama Moose's big head bobbed safely to the surface just ahead of her calves. Mama Moose swam nicely as three moose heads, their bulky bodies underwater, moved silently toward the far-off point where the windows of a lone forest cabin glimmered in the afternoon sun of late summer.

Hannah figured she knew this stretch of water pretty well. Often, with only Hunter as company, she took one of Papa's canoes around Beaver Island. With her casting rod, she would catch catfish, perch, and pickerel among the cattails in the little coves. This spot, much shallower than the rest of the lake, had a rock-strewn sand bottom where sassy sunfish, beautiful bluegills, and tiny shiners darted away from her paddle as she glided along.

"Hey!" Hannah cried. "Let's check it out ourselves!"

"Arf!" Hunter agreed.

"Let's see, fellers," Hannah said as they splashed into Moosehead Lake. "I'll just bet.... I'll bet the cabin owner's got a jeep road, or at least a horse trail, into Laketon." Hannah's brain swam with thoughts of riding Ebony through the deep forest to Laketon, where Uncle Joe Boudreau could take the horse to Skowhegan Fair in his new pickup truck. All they had to do was rent a horse trailer.

A school of bluegills cast their shadows on the lake's sandy bottom. Hunter spied them and leaped after them.

"Crazy dog," Hannah chuckled. Hunter splashed farther out, where his legs no longer touched bottom. He began to paddle, enjoying a chance to cool off.

"Hup, Ebony!" Hannah slapped the reins. "Let's you'n me follow him." Ebony was used to the water. Hannah had watched more than once when Papa and their only island neighbor, Sam Sampson, had used Ebony to move sunken logs and rocks to clear the waterfront at Beaver Lodge. But she didn't know whether Ebony could swim like the moose. Hannah figured she'd better ask her parents before she *really* tried to find out. She decided that there would be no harm in letting Ebony splash out a hundred yards or so, though. That way, she'd have a better idea what he could do when she talked to Mama and Papa later.

Hunter soon tired of swimming and went back

toward shore. Ebony was in up over his belly now, and Hannah's boots were filling with lake water. But with the excitement she was feeling, she forgot her boots and wet socks.

"Easy, feller." Hannah spoke quietly, urging Ebony on, yet not letting him hurry like the moose had done. "The channel's quite a ways out there, yet. It'll be all right, boy."

When Hannah had crossed the old logging tug-boat channel in a canoe, she had been able to see the bottom until she got to where it dropped off into the inky blackness of the deep lake. But Ebony's hooves now stirred up bottom dirt. So Hannah had to judge where the channel was by how far she had ridden. She glanced back at Beaver Island. "Far enough, big feller. Whoa!"

Ebony halted and whinnied nervously.

"Hush, Ebony!" Hannah didn't want to attract attention, and she knew sound would carry across the smooth, silent lake clear to the cabin.

The cabin—that's why she had taken Ebony into the lake in the first place. When Mr. Morris built his cabin, he had cut down a few pines and firs, making a clearing. Hannah had spied an old pickup truck parked in the rear. It was beat-up, like the one Walt bounced around Beaver Island in.

"They've got a jeep road, all right," Hannah laughed, noticing the old truck. "And Ebony, big guy, you're soon gonna try it out! Let's go talk to Mama. Hup!"

Ebony took a step, turning back toward Beaver Island. Suddenly horse and saddle melted away beneath Hannah. Ebony was in over his head! Moosehead Lake grabbed Hannah's boots with strong, watery fingers, dragging Hannah into the deep, black channel. "Help!" She managed just one word as her head went under. Hannah would drown in the Maine wilderness with no one to help.

Hannah held her breath as she tread water. Her nose was barely out of the water, and her boots wouldn't let her swim. She knew that yelling would only cause her to swallow water and drown. Ebony's head was out of the water now, but Hannah was still in deep trouble as she fought to yank her boots off.

Suddenly a squirming, furry, wet hound appeared directly in front of Hannah. Hannah grabbed his haunches, kicking with both her feet, gulping air as she hung on. *If only Hunter can keep our heads up while I kick my boots off. Jesus, help me!* Hannah prayed silently, remembering how Peter had cried out to Jesus when he sank into the Sea of Galilee.

Finally, Hannah felt her boots slip free. Without Hunter's help, she swam toward shore. Hannah's toes caught the gravel ridge at the edge of the channel, and her feet reached bottom again.

When she came up out of the water, her clothes hung heavily on her. She went straight to Ebony, who had reached shore before her, and tethered him to a tree.

She squeezed water out of her braid. "At least you didn't get spooked and run off across the island without me."

Hannah shivered. "Lucky," she said, looking at Ebony and Hunter, "you fellers got fur!"

Hannah went behind the brush pile, out of sight of the cabin across the lake, and wrung out her clothes. Hunter shook himself, spraying Hannah. "Cut that out!" she said more gruffly than she had intended. Hunter, after all, had helped save her.

"Thank you, Jesus," Hannah breathed for the fiftieth time. She knew that someone besides Hunter had been looking out for her. She hadn't been so scared in a long time.

And now how would she explain her wet clothes and missing boots to Mama? To say the least, it had been *unwise* for her to go out so far when she couldn't see the bottom.

Suddenly, Hannah began to laugh. She looked at Ebony, standing where she had tethered him, his black fur wet. What was she thinking, worrying about all these things? Ebony had just proven that he could swim.

"Ebony can swim!" she shouted into the woods, laughing. "Ebony can swim!"

*Chapter Three*

# Only Fantasy?

Hannah smiled to herself as she and Hunter slipped in the back door of Beaver Lodge. She pulled off her dirty socks, grimy from walking from the pasture with no boots, then slipped barefoot up the back stairs.

Hannah had left her old riding boots, the ones she wore for barn chores, at the bottom of the channel, but she didn't mind. Hannah, in fact, had to stifle a chuckle as the idea she had gotten from watching the moose swim now swam inside her excited mind.

"SQUAWK!" *I wish Papa would fix that ol' stair tread,* Hannah fretted. The front staircase, used by the tourist guests, was carpeted and did not squeak.

"That you, Hannah?" Mama called from the kitchen.

"Yes. Gotta hurry!"

"You're right," Mama softly admonished. "Molly's waiting to be milked."

"I know, Mama. Gotta change my clothes first."

Once in her room, Hannah dug deep into her

21

closet. She finally fished out a pair of old L. L. Bean work boots that had first been Walt's, then hers. *I need a hat, too,* Hannah considered, half smiling. Her straw cowgirl hat had floated off when she took the dunking, but Hannah couldn't care less. With fall weather coming, she wanted a real felt Western hat—especially since she now figured she could enter the Texas rodeo. Hannah yanked on dry jeans and an old sweatshirt. She clapped an old baseball cap on backwards and bent to yank a boot on.

The leather of the boot's top was stiff, and Hannah hauled—hard. "Ouch!" The boot slipped on all of a sudden, and Hannah's toes hurt as they curled under inside the too-short rubber bottom. Hannah stared. The leather-and-rubber Bean boots could *not* have shrunk, even after nearly a year in the closet. But the boots used to be *too big!*

Hannah smiled grimly. Three shoe sizes in eight months. "It seems like I've let my stirrups down a couple of times this summer, too," she said half aloud. She took a breath and looked at herself in the long mirror on her closet door. "Oh, well!" Hannah winced and yanked the other boot on.

She clomped downstairs and out to the barn.

"Hannah, you must be *crippled* in those old boots," Mama said when Hannah hobbled from the barn into the lodge kitchen nearly an hour later with a pail of Molly's fresh milk.

"I know, Mama," Hannah said quietly. "I can get a pair of cheap rubber barn boots in Laketon tomorrow when I take the boat to get the mail." Hannah set the milk pail on the sideboard, then plopped into a chair to tug her boots from her aching feet.

"Those old riding boots—the ones you wear everywhere—they're big enough."

"Yeah." *Mama's getting too close,* Hannah thought. "When's Papa getting home?"

"He's been delayed. The tourists from New York he went to meet in the boat phoned from Skowhegan. They're running about an hour behind. We'll serve them all supper later."

"Oh." Hannah stood and reached for the milk strainer.

"Hannah?"

*Uh-oh.* "Yes, Mama?"

"Where *are* your riding boots?"

"At...at the bottom of the lake."

"Lake! But you went horseback riding! Did someone leave a boat over there?"

"No. I took Ebony..."

"And you fell off! What if Ebony had fallen in? A horse can't swim, you know!"

"Well, we made it, anyway." Hannah smiled wryly. She now knew very well that a horse could swim, but it didn't seem a good time to frighten Mama with the whole story. Mama had learned to enjoy life on the edge of the forest since moving to their island in Moosehead Lake from the city of Skowhegan. But still, she became nervous when Hannah or Walt got what Mama called "too close to nature."

Mama frowned, then smiled and shook her head. "I guess when kids grow up they have to try their wings. You're safer in the country than dodging cars on a bike in the city, I guess. Just be careful you don't fly too high till you're ready, okay? Think things through."

"Okay, Mama." Hannah smiled, relieved.

"Now please go put on your sneakers and a clean dress. I can use some help getting supper for the guests."

"Sure, Mama." Hannah hurried upstairs, her thoughts running in several directions at once. *Papa says I'm "almost a woman." He also says Mama is finding my growing up a bit hard to take.* Hannah sighed. *We've sure had a lot more disagreements than usual lately,*

"I hope Papa understands," Hannah said to Hunter, who had curled up on her bed. "Life just goes on and on fer you, doesn't it, feller?"

Hunter lifted one sleepy eyelid. "Ooh-ooo," he agreed, and fell back to sleep at once.

"Ebony can swim, Papa!"

Papa smiled and peered at Hannah over his reading glasses. "Most horses can swim. God made 'em that way."

Mama stared. "Stop teasing me, Harry. That's... that's just not possible. Horses don't have fins or even paws to paddle with. Next it'll be chickens diving like ducks!"

"Do I perceive that there's more to this story than a disagreement over the aquatic abilities of the equestrian species?" Papa chuckled.

"Harry, this is no time to use more big words than Webster has dictionaries," Mama objected. "Hannah lost her riding boots in the lake this afternoon, but she never told me she was out in that old tug channel back of the island."

"Oh? Sounds like you pushed things a little too far."

"Yes, Papa. But you'd never have guessed—Ebony swims like a seal."

"Hannah, this is no time for jokes!" Mama scolded.

"Mama, I'm not joking. Please!"

"Tell me about it, Hannah," Papa said pleasantly.

Hannah began at the beginning. Detail by detail, she told Mama and Papa all the events of that exciting afternoon.

"Wow!" Papa exclaimed as Hannah finished. "Your mother has every right to be concerned. And now you want to take Ebony across the channel and ride him around the lake to enter the Texas rodeo?" He shook his head, smiling, a shake and a smile that said, "Crazy idea, but it just might work."

"That's one big proposal," Papa sighed. "That old logging tugboat channel is deep, but quite narrow—maybe only a hundred feet. Ebony could wade up to his belly the rest of the way. Trouble is, once we got him to the mainland back there, he'd still be way back in the woods—if he would even cooperate to swim."

Mama shook her head.

"Papa," Hannah urged, "Mr. Morris, who lives in that cabin—he didn't hesitate when you asked to hook into his phone line, did he?"

"No, I don't suppose he did. The line cost him a bit of money, and he was glad to have us help pay for it."

"And he's got an old truck over there—so there's *gotta* be a road into Laketon." Hannah looked at Mama and Papa. "It has to work. I just read in the rodeo brochure that winners get to compete at the big rodeo in Texas—they get plane tickets and everything."

"Oh?" Papa said. "Well, Texas is a bit far off for us. You're still thinking of how to get Ebony off the island."

"Swimming horses!" Mama was plainly amazed. "What'll it be next—trotting oysters?"

"That bit of fantasy is from Lewis Carroll's fiction," Papa sighed.

"It's from *Alice in Wonderland*," Hannah agreed. She began to fear that her plan was not going to work after all. "But this is *not* fantasy!"

"I know," Papa said. He looked earnestly at Mama, then at Hannah. "I understand—we both understand. But we need to pray about it—and sleep on it." Papa glanced at the mantel clock, then reached for his Bible.

"Check out the *National Geographic* when you get a chance," Mama said the next morning. "The one on the mantel. I read it last night after you went to bed."

Hannah had just finished pouring a late-for-breakfast guest his final cup of coffee, and she wanted to dig into her schoolwork so she could start thinking about the rodeo. "Something for my history lesson, Mama?"

"Natural history—whatever. I left a bookmark in it."

Hannah sat in the big leather easy chair by the fireplace and flipped the magazine open to an article on wild mustangs of Spain. One photo showed wild horses swimming between islands in the Atlantic Ocean. These Spanish islands, said the article, were nearly five miles apart. "Thank You, Jesus," Hannah whispered quietly.

Hannah replaced the *Geographic* on the big, hand-carved pine log mantel above Beaver Lodge's fireplace. She slipped into the kitchen and hugged Mama. "I'm sorry, Mama," Hannah said. "I know I used poor judgement when I took Ebony near that old channel."

"You were excited. I don't blame you." Mama kissed Hannah's forehead. "I learn something new about country life almost every day."

"Does this mean I *can* take Ebony across the channel?"

"It means that your father is going to see what he can work out." Mama pointed toward the dock, where Papa was helping guests take their seats in his big boat. "Now run down to the dock with this thermos of coffee!"

"Papa, did you see that article in *National Geographic*?" Hannah asked moments later as she passed Papa the gallon thermos and cups for the boatload of guests. "Does that mean...?"

Papa smiled to see Hannah so excited. "I'll definitely look into it. I'm taking our tourists up Eight Mile Brook to see nature up close this morning. I'll check with Mr. Morris on the way back. But don't get your hopes up."

"I wish I could go with you to talk to him."

"I know you do, but we'll be gone all morning, and you need to do your schoolwork."

All morning as Hannah worked, she kept thinking about Mr. Morris. Would he say yes? She wanted to be there to explain how important it was that Ebony get to the rodeo, but she knew that Papa's going was best. If he didn't go on his way back, he might not have another chance right away. And if Mr. Morris did say yes, how far would it be on his jeep road to Laketon? In the middle of problem twenty Hannah thought of how to find out: She would look in Papa's hunting-trail map. Hannah shoved these thoughts from her mind long enough to finish her algebra problems, all thirty-two of them.

Hungry for lunch but too curious to wait, Hannah went straight to Papa's study. Just as she'd hoped, the trail map was resting on top of his guide-books on his bookshelf. Hannah spread the map out on top of a bunch of papers and the little pho-tocopier Papa kept on his desk for business. There was the point where Mr. Morris's cabin was. And there was Laketon. Her finger found the trail that connected them. Seven miles! That wasn't far at all. Her mind spun. She had to think of everything. Once Ebony made it to Laketon—and Hannah was sure he would, he just had to—how would he get to the fair in Skowhegan? He couldn't walk there.

Hannah turned this new problem over in her head as she wandered into the kitchen. Maybe Uncle Joe...

"What are you thinking about?" Mama laughed.

"Huh?" Hannah realized she had been standing in the middle of the kitchen staring blindly out the window. She had come into the kitchen to see whether Mama needed help with lunch or whether all the guests had gone with Papa—and to get some-thing to eat for herself. "Ebony," Hannah said. "Do you know it's only seven miles from Mr. Morris's to Laketon?"

Mama was sitting at the kitchen table with some paperwork. She smiled, stretching her hands toward the ceiling. "That's good news. I've been working on these bills longer than I intended."

"Are the guests all gone?"

"Yes," Mama said. "I was thinking we could just make ourselves some sandwiches."

Hannah nodded absently. "If we rented a horse trailer, do you think Uncle Joe would haul Ebony to Skowhegan with his truck?"

Mama laughed. "You and this rodeo. Call him and find out. You won't rest until you do. But Hannah?"

"Yes?" Hannah didn't like the sound of this.

"It's good you're thinking positively and that you're thinking ahead about what you need to do. Just keep in mind that this is complicated, and for it to work it'll take the cooperation of a lot of people. Understand that it may not work like you would like it to."

"I know," Hannah said out loud. But really, she wasn't letting herself think about that at all. It *had* to work.

*Chapter Four*

# Flying High

By the time Hannah sat down that night with Mama, Papa, and Walt to talk about the rodeo, she was crazy with anticipation. Uncle Joe had agreed to haul Ebony with his truck if she could arrange a horse trailer rental. But she hadn't been able to get the whole story from Papa, just that Mr. Morris was very nice and had agreed, but...

"But what?" Hannah asked now. "If he agreed to help us, what's the problem?"

"There are still some logistics to be worked out," Papa said.

"Logistics?" Hannah knew that that word had something to do with moving things around in tough circumstances. She did not like the sound of this. "But Mr. Morris has a jeep trail, doesn't he? I found it on your forest map."

"Sure he does," Papa agreed. "But Mr. Morris uses his trail directly into Laketon only in winter, when the swamp through there is frozen solid enough to drive on. The rest of the year, Ebony would sink into the muck."

"So what do we do?" Hannah asked. "There has to be another way."

"There is," Papa said. "Twelve miles in the opposite direction, to reach Northwoods Logging Company's good road. From there it's another sixty miles clear around Moosehead Lake to get to Uncle Joe's in Laketon, Mr. Morris told me."

"Sixty miles!" Walt whistled.

"So," Hannah groaned, "we've got to go *clear* around the big lake. And I thought the whole thing was only going to be seven miles."

"Unless horses can walk on soft muck as well as swim," Mama agreed.

"Getting to Laketon is still doable," Papa put in.

"You mean, maybe have Uncle Joe drive around the lake for Ebony the long way?" Hannah asked.

"Or ride him around," Walt added. "I'd love it."

Hannah shot a warning look at her older brother. She knew very well that riding seventy-two miles in one day would be too much for any horse, even such a big stallion as Ebony.

"Probably we can figure something out," Papa said. "Meanwhile, you may use the lower pasture to practice barrel racing. Just use good judgement so as not to disturb our guests."

"Some of them may find your practice entertaining, though," Mama teased.

"I'll charge 'em extra for ringside seats." Hannah laughed.

Walt frowned. "But what about the application deadlines? The applications have to get there by next week."

"You can send yours in, no problem, Walt. I'm sure we can find a way for you to practice." Mama looked at Hannah. "How much did you say it costs to apply?"

"Twenty-five dollars each," Hannah said.

Mama and Papa looked at each other. "You too, Hannah," Mama said. "Go ahead and apply, and we'll do our best to make it happen. We don't want you to miss the deadline."

Hannah jumped up and kissed Papa's bristly cheek, because he was the closest. "You guys are the best!"

"Hang onto your money, Hannah," Mama said later. "You'll need some new riding boots for that barrel-racing contest." Mama had just written a check for fifty dollars to the Texas Mesquite Rodeo Association—twenty-five dollars for Hannah's entry fee and twenty-five for Walt's. "We can be thankful we've had fairly steady income from the lodge. Has Caylin said how her dad's job search is going? It's been many weeks now since he lost his job."

"Uh-uh. She hasn't. Thanks, Mama."

Hannah took the check to her desk in the living room. Carefully, she addressed a long envelope to "Texas Mesquite Rodeo Association, Dallas, Texas." She slipped Mama's fifty-dollar check inside, along with Walt's application.

"Walt," Hannah said, checking her own application for mistakes. "It says I've got to be thirteen. I'm twelve."

"So? The rodeo isn't until October 26. You're thirteen October 17. Put down thirteen."

"Would that be honest?"

"You want to be in the contest, don't you?"

"Ye-es," Hannah agreed. She looked at where she'd already written "12" and placed an asterisk beside it. She put another asterisk at the bottom of the form. Beside it, Hannah wrote, "My birthday is Oct. 17, when I'll be 13."

Hannah was just placing the envelope with her entry form on the pile of mail to go to Laketon the next day when the phone rang. "Beaver Lodge," she said brightly.

"Hi, Han—"

"Caylin! Guess what? You'll never guess! I'm gonna be in the rodeo. Mama just wrote the check."

"Good. I knew you'd find a way. Hey, Han? You lived in Skowhegan once, right?"

"Skowhegan? Yeah. That's where the rodeo's gonna be." Hannah twirled around in her stocking feet, the phone cord wrapping twice around her. "Guess how Ebony's getting to the mainland." Hannah couldn't believe she was actually going to the rodeo.

"You found someone with a boat big enough to haul him?"

"No, silly. No boat. Ebony's gonna swim!"

"Yeah, sure," Caylin laughed.

"I'm serious," Hannah said.

"But he's a *horse*. And it's like, a couple of miles across!"

"Not from the back of our island, it isn't."

"Oh? Well, I'm glad it'll work. Now if I could just get over this sore throat I've been having so it doesn't hurt to sing. Oh, Han, won't it be fun if we *both* compete at the fair? The person who wins the Miss Lakeland pageant competes at the fair for Texas Mesquite Miss of Maine." Caylin's voice dropped. "But I'm not counting on winning. I'm not sure about anything. My dad—"

"Of course you'll win," Hannah said. "Oh, I haven't told you, have I—the barrel race winner gets to go compete in Texas. Can you believe it? You'll be home in the morning, won't you? I found this article on swimming horses and everything. Maybe I can show you. Mama would probably let me do the mail run tomorrow. We need to mail our applications in."

"Sure, come by," Caylin said. "Maybe we can talk about it later, okay?"

"Sure. Bye." Hannah put the phone down. Talk about what later? she wondered. She suddenly remembered that Caylin had called her. *Was she talking about the rodeo or something else?* Hannah shrugged. *Probably the rodeo.*

Hannah peered out the kitchen window and up the hill to where Ebony was a silver ghost in the moonlight as he munched his grass in the nighttime pasture. "Rest now, Ebony," she said half aloud. "'Cause starting tomorrow or Monday or whenever we find some barrels, you and me are gonna race to win. We're gonna rule!"

*Why can't Mama ever trust me to do anything right?* Hannah wondered as she dropped their applications to the Texas rodeo in the mail slot at the post office. She noticed that the envelope had been cut open, then taped back up. Hannah had taken Papa's boat to Laketon for the mail, just as she had hoped.

"Why don't you take an hour or so and watch one of your Uncle Joe's rodeo tapes?" Mama had suggested as Hannah left.

"That's a good idea, only I was going to go to Caylin's." Hannah shrugged. "It's Saturday. I guess I can do both."

"Don't be gone too long," Mama said. "You need to get a head start on some of your schoolwork so nothing falls behind with all the rodeo preparation. I know how you get caught up in things."

Hannah wasn't happy about it at first. She had hoped to spend maybe the whole day with Caylin. But she knew Mama was right, and she agreed to be back by lunchtime. She stopped to get Caylin on her way to Uncle Joe's, and together the girls trooped through the gate Uncle Joe had put in his backyard fence so his family could visit with Caylin's family, the Coulsons, and not have to walk clear around the block.

Hannah and Caylin watched Uncle Joe's video of the state of Wyoming junior champion barrel rider for what seemed like a hundred times. Uncle Joe had taped it the week before from the Mesquite rodeo program on his cable TV, and it had some pretty good action shots of champion Kennie MacKenzie and her horse. Uncle Joe came in from his garage as Hannah began to replay the video of the barrel race.

"It's less than twenty seconds, Uncle Joe—the part I need to watch." She began the tape again. The girl on horseback slapped her hat across her painted mustang's withers, then bent across its neck, talking to her horse as it raced off.

"See...see how she guides it with her knees!" Uncle Joe was getting excited now. "I've worked with plenty of hosses. I *know* hosses," he exclaimed in his French-accented English. "You've got to *become* part of ze hoss if you're going to win."

The scene shifted to the lighted sign at the end of the Texas Mesquite Rodeo's big indoor arena: "15.2," the sign read, and Hannah knew that meant seconds. "Another great performance in horsemanship for our young rider from Wyoming!" the announcer called over the cheers of the crowd.

Hannah suddenly knew what she wanted. She

wanted to be as good as Kennie MacKenzie. She and Uncle Joe replayed the tape, chattering with excitement about the barrel-racing contest.

"Hannah has quite the plan for getting Ebony to the mainland, doesn't she?" Uncle Joe said.

Caylin nodded from her spot on the couch.

"Ebony will swim across," Uncle Joe explained. "He'll need to be led on a rope from a boat to keep him from getting frightened, of course." Uncle Joe's kind, dark eyes twinkled with excitement.

"Like they crossed the river with horses in *Little House*," Hannah added. "Well, there's still some *logistics* to work out, Papa says." Hannah laughed and rolled her father's big word over her tongue. "Like how we're going to get him around to Laketon." She looked at Uncle Joe. "I haven't talked to you since I found out that the seven-mile trail is a swamp until winter. We have to go all the way around the lake. Twelve miles on a trail and then sixty on the Northwoods logging road."

Uncle Joe's eyes widened. "That's a mighty big logistic. It would take nearly all day."

Hannah sighed. "Yeah." Uncle Joe had already promised to bring Ebony from Laketon to Skowhegan, where the rodeo was. Hannah had been hoping he'd offer to meet them at the logging road.

Uncle Joe was thinking. "I don't know of any other way into town from Mr. Morris's point."

"If we rode him to the end of the twelve-mile trail," Hannah said, "could you pick him up from there? Would you be able to haul him on the logging road? Please, Uncle Joe?"

Uncle Joe smiled. "You're determined, aren't you? I like that about you, and yes, I'll talk to your Papa to see if that would work. Are there any other *logistics* you need to talk to me about?"

"Not now."

Uncle Joe smiled at Caylin. "With you in the pageant and Hannah in the rodeo, we're going to have two stars. I know from hearing you sing at church that you have a very special voice."

"Thanks," Caylin said.

"Wouldn't it be awesome if we both won?" Hannah said. "Papa said I could practice in the pasture. But when the rodeo gets closer—when Ebony and I get better—we're going to need a better place."

"How about the riding club?" Caylin suggested. "They have horse stables, don't they?"

"The club doesn't even have stalls enough for its own members. I checked that out myself yesterday," Uncle Joe explained.

"Really?" Hannah hadn't thought of the riding club.

"Our garage used to be a horse stable, Joe," said Aunt Theresa, who had been listening from the kitchen. She brought Joe a cup of steaming coffee.

"Floor's rotted through back in the stalls." Uncle Joe shook his head. "Besides, every spare inch is crammed full o' old furniture waiting for me to fix up to sell."

"There's always a yard sale, Joe," Aunt Theresa said.

Hannah eyed her uncle. "The stable would be perfect. Only where would we practice?"

Caylin looked at her funny.

"What?" Hannah asked.

Caylin just shrugged.

Uncle Joe took a drink of his coffee. "I'm not sure what of that stuff I'm ready to sell."

Hannah hit rewind to watch the tape of Kennie MacKenzie one more time.

※　※　※　※　※　※　※

"Ebony just wants to trot, Walt," Hannah fumed. "He's *got* to gallop." Hannah was nearly in tears.

"That's 'cause he's been taught to race in a harness," Walt said. "You've seen those sulky races at the Skowhegan Fairgrounds? It's because he was taught to trot that Papa bought Ebony, to trot on the ice and pull a sleigh."

"I know!" Hannah wiped her nose on the sleeve of her Western chambray shirt. "But Ebony *can* gallop. When I give him rein on the woods road, he gallops clear across the island."

"Then—just give him rein!"

"But he'll kick the barrels over! Or go way wide around them. I've been practicing every day this week, and we haven't gotten anywhere."

"Let me try." Walt grabbed the bridle.

"All right." Hannah slid from the saddle.

"Yee-hah!" Walt slapped the reins, then let them go slack.

Ebony shot across the pasture at a gallop, like in the woods, headed for the first barrel. He overshot it, but Walt turned him wide around it and headed straight across to the second. The second and third corners Ebony turned too tight and knocked the barrels over. Walt rode Ebony fast back to the starting point, even though it had clearly been a losing run.

Walt reined him in. "See—he gallops, too!"

"Yeah," Hannah panted, running across the pasture to set up the two fallen barrels. "But he doesn't have much control."

Walt grinned. "One barrel's still standing. Maybe if you get him used to galloping through the course, then you can work on control. One thing at a time."

Hannah jogged back across the scrubby grass and dirt patches of the lower pasture. She and

Ebony should have been practicing in dirt, but the pasture was the best they could do on the island. Eventually, she would somehow need to find a way to practice on the mainland. But she couldn't just sit around *waiting* for that.

"Hey, Walt." Hannah pulled a rodeo pamphlet from her shirt pocket. Now would be a good time to get her brother to help her get the barrels set up the exact distances and angles.

Walt swung down from the saddle. "You gonna try it now?"

"Not yet. Help me get the course set up right." Hannah flipped through the pamphlet put out by the rodeo until she found the pages on barrel racing. "I've got it close, I think, but timing's gonna be everything. I want us to practice right. See here, we have the barrels at the three points of a triangle like they should be, but I haven't measured out the distances between them."

Walt studied the diagram.

"That's a cool way to describe it," he said. "It says you ride a *cloverleaf* pattern around the barrels."

"That is a good way to describe it." Hannah toed a line in a patch of dirt. "This will be the starting gate. I'll find a flag or something to put here later. We'll ride from here and back to here."

Walt went to Papa's shop to find a measuring tape. Finally he and Hannah had the distances measured and the barrels placed.

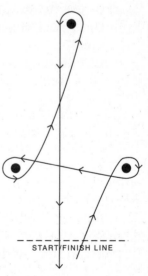

START/FINISH LINE

Across the pasture, Hannah grabbed Ebony's saddle horn and swung into the saddle.

"Want me to time you?" Walt asked, back at the starting line.

Hannah shook her head and spurred Ebony with her heels. "Let me get the technique down first. One thing at a time, like you said," she called back.

Approaching the first corner, Hannah reined Ebony in too soon and made him turn too tight, and he knocked over the first barrel. Hannah overcompensated. Ebony was so wide on the other two corners he was in no danger of knocking them over. He was just too slow. But at least he was galloping.

Just then Papa pulled his boat up to the dock from taking a couple of guests to their car in Laketon. He carried the mail to them, and he grinned as he passed Walt and Hannah each an unopened, long, first-class envelope from Dallas, Texas.

"I'm in!" Walt yelled, quickly reading his letter from the Texas Mesquite Rodeo Association. "I'm in the rodeo!"

Hannah read her letter silently. Tears spilled down her freckled cheeks as she passed the open letter back to Papa:

*Dear Ms. Hannah Parmenter,*

the letter began,

*We regret to inform you that the minimum age for participation in the Texas Mesquite Rodeo's riding contests is thirteen. Your application states that you are twelve years old....*"

A check for twenty-five dollars floated out of the envelope as Hannah dropped it to the ground and drooped in her saddle.

# Chapter Five

# Left Out

"Local Girls to Compete," said the headline on the back page of the Friday afternoon weekly *Laketon Gazette*. Hannah had refused at first to read it when Papa had brought it home the day before—at the same time he had brought the letters from the rodeo association. She stared grimly at the row of photos along the bottom. There was pretty Caylin, right in the middle. *Of course!* Hannah brooded. *Caylin's in the middle of everything.*

Hannah tossed the newspaper onto the porch glider and leaned back in the old, high-backed porch rocker. She knew she should be happy for her friend, and she wanted to be. But how could she be happy—why *should* she be happy—when her nothing was going right? First, the letter saying that she was too young. Then she began wishing she'd entered the Miss Lakeland pageant. But the deadline for that was long past.

*Not that I really wanted to enter,* Hannah told herself. *I just thought...* Tears slid down her cheeks. She wanted to be in *something*. The girl who won the Miss Lakeland contest would get to compete in the big pageant at the rodeo.

Hannah's head hurt as she thought about how yesterday, just before she got the letter, she had finally felt like she would be able to train Ebony. Now it was all pointless—a sick joke. Mama had called the rodeo right away that morning to see whether they understood Hannah's note that she would be thirteen by the time of the rodeo, but it was Saturday, and all she got was voice mail.

Mama stuck her head out the screen door. "Hannah, I need you to run to Laketon in the motorboat. Aunt Theresa has baked some raspberry pies I need to serve our guests."

"I don't feel like going anywhere."

Mama came outside and sat beside Hannah. "I know it doesn't seem like it, but getting out might help you feel better." Mama put her arm around Hannah's shoulders. "I'll do what I can to see if I can clear your age with the rodeo committee. Like Papa said last night, maybe it's just a misunderstanding. Meanwhile, I'd think twice about quitting practice." Mama smiled. "Your determination is one of your best qualities, you know."

Hannah nodded. The lump in her throat grew bigger by the second, and her eyes welled with tears. Sometimes, when she was trying not to cry, kind, comforting words like Mama's made the tears come.

"How come everything's so easy for Caylin?" she asked quietly.

"Caylin? Oh." Mama saw the newspaper on the porch glider. "Are things easy for her? How easy do you think it is for her to have her dad unemployed and to not know where he might find a job?"

"I don't know. She hasn't talked about it much."

"Hasn't she? Or have you just not given her a chance, with all your excitement about the rodeo?"

Hannah shrugged. What did Mama mean? Caylin could say anything she wanted.

Mama stood up. "You better get going. Just remember that things are seldom what they seem, Hannah."

*Yeah,* Hannah thought. It had seemed like she was going to be in the rodeo. Now she wasn't.

"My dad tries not to worry, but I can tell he does. He tries to joke like he used to, but the other night I woke up and he was sitting in the living room in the dark. Now he had an interview in Skowhe—oh—hi, Hannah," Caylin said. She was playing checkers with Uncle Joe at the dining room table when Hannah came in from the kitchen. Caylin had had to leave her grandparents in Connecticut when her family moved to Maine a little more than a year earlier, so she had adopted Uncle Joe as her grandpa.

"Hi," Hannah said. She had been able to tell from the kitchen she was going to interrupt Caylin and Uncle Joe's conversation, so finally she just walked in. She stood there feeling awkward. "I came to get the pies. Aunt Theresa went to find some cardboard to pack them with."

"Have a seat," Uncle Joe said. "We need to talk to you about Ebony."

Hannah sat down at the table. "Ebony?"

"Yeah," Caylin said, "I'm working on Uncle Joe. I've agreed to help clean his stable-garage out."

"Gotta have a stall for ze hoss, *non?*" Uncle Joe chuckled. "We still have to figure out where to practice, but one thing at a time."

"Yeah?" Hannah leaned her chair back on two legs and let it fall back down with a thump onto the hardwood floor.

Uncle Joe opened his mouth. "I know," Hannah said. "Aunt Theresa doesn't like it when I do that. I forgot."

"Well?" Uncle Joe said. "What do you think? Don't you want to bring Ebony?"

"Of course I do." Hannah's eyes rested on Uncle Joe's stack of rodeo videos.

"Something bugging you?" Caylin asked.

"Me? No, I'm fine."

"Hey, you've got to see my pageant dress." Caylin took a drink of her ice water. "My throat's still sore, can you believe it? I got the dress yesterday. My mom said she'd help me put my hair up." She piled her red curls on top of her head. "Something like this."

"Perfect," Uncle Joe said.

"As if you'd know," Caylin laughed, her blue eyes sparkling.

"If you'll excuse me, ladies," Uncle Joe said, "I think I'll get myself a cup of coffee."

Caylin reached across the table for a sheet of music. "Of course, my performance is the important thing. Aunt Theresa promised to play the piano for me when I sing."

Hannah flicked over a stack of red checkers. "Great."

"What's your problem?" Caylin asked.

"Nobody cares what my problem is. And I don't have to tell."

"If you don't want to tell, why are you making it so obvious something's wrong? Besides, I care. It's me, Caylin—your friend, remember?"

"Want to come spend the night?" Hannah found

herself asking. "We'll bring you back in the morning in time for church."

Caylin twisted a curl around her finger, studying Hannah. "Sure. I love spending the night. I'll go ask my mom—and I'll bring my pageant dress."

"And I'll check with Mama on the phone, then help Aunt Theresa pack the pies."

When the girls went into the kitchen, Aunt Theresa was busily cutting cardboard into disks to place between the pies in a basket.

"I'm going to go with Hannah," Caylin said.

Uncle Joe laughed. "Well, look at that. Hannah takes my checker partner away without even asking."

"Thanks, Joe," Caylin said, knowing he was teasing. "Talk to you later?"

"Later," he smiled. "Anytime."

"I know you heard me tell Uncle Joe about my dad." Caylin was steadying the baskets of pies so the boat ride wouldn't ruin them.

"Did you say he had an interview in Skowhegan?"

"Uh-huh. I'm afraid we might have to move, and we've only been in Laketon a year. Oh, Hannah, what if he doesn't get a job at all?"

"Of course he will," Hannah said. Even though Caylin hadn't lived in Laketon long, Caylin and Hannah had become best friends. Hannah didn't want to think about Caylin's moving. Not when she was already upset about the rodeo.

"Well, he might not get a job," Caylin said. "Or he might have to look for one even farther away than Skowhegan, and then for sure we'd have to move.

And now I have to go to the doctor because my throat won't get better. Doctors cost tons of money. It feels like I've been sick practically forever."

Hannah's head ached. The last thing she needed today was to listen to someone worry and complain. Since they got in the boat, Caylin hadn't even asked her what was wrong.

"And being in the pageant is costing money now, too." Caylin's dress was protected in a plastic garment bag.

Hannah didn't want to hear another word about the pageant. "At least you're still in the pageant." Hannah pulled the boat up to the Beaver Lodge's dock. "I'm not even in the rodeo."

"You're not?"

"Uh-uh. I'll show you inside." She wondered whether the rodeo association had called Mama back yet.

No sooner had Hannah and Caylin trudged into Beaver Lodge's kitchen carrying Aunt Theresa's pies than Walt's voice crackled on the walkie-talkie above the sink. "Ma, I'm just about out of chain saw gas. Can Hannah ride over on Ebony with a two-gallon can?"

Hannah frowned at Caylin as Mama talked with Walt. Walt was cutting firewood on the back of the island. Hannah did *not* wish to ride off to help her brother. It made her mad for Walt to call right when she had invited a friend over. Of course, she had to admit he didn't know that.

"Mama," Hannah protested, "Caylin's here."

"I don't mind," Caylin said. "We could ride over double, couldn't we?"

"You could—"

"Mama," Hannah said again. She didn't even feel like riding Ebony right now. It made her think about the rodeo she wouldn't be riding in.

Mama seemed to understand. "Walt, Hannah has company right now. Why don't you come on home for lunch?"

Hannah motioned for Caylin to follow her upstairs.

"How come you're not in the rodeo?" Caylin asked.

"I'll show you."

In Hannah's room, Caylin dropped her backpack to the floor and hung her dress bag over the door. Hannah showed Caylin the letter from Texas and explained how careful she'd been to explain her age.

"Hannah, that really stinks! They *can't* do this to you!" Caylin threw the letter on Hannah's bed.

"But they *are!*"

"But you *told* them when your birthday is—now it's past the deadline. "Didn't your parents even try?"

"Of course, but we just found out yesterday. Mama called them, but we just got a recording." Hannah shrugged helplessly.

"You should call them again."

"Mama says it's rude to call again without giving them time to call us back. But c'mon downstairs. I didn't get to ask her if they called while I was gone."

"No call back yet," Mama said, wringing out a dishrag in the kitchen sink. "But I'll call again Monday afternoon if they haven't called by then." She handed the rag to Hannah and motioned at the guest tables in the dining room. "Papa will be back with the guests soon. If you'll just set the tables for me, you can do what you want with the rest of the day."

Hannah went into the other room.

"If you'll show me where the dishes are, I'll help," Caylin offered.

"Right here," Mama said. "How was your father's interview yesterday?"

Hannah strained to hear over the clatter of plates and silverware. Even Mama knew about the interview?

"He thought it went well," Caylin was saying now. "He's really trying to trust God and not worry, but it's hard. My mom and I went with him to Skowhegan and went shopping. I picked out my pageant dress. Mom said they weren't going to sacrifice that. Dad agreed. He said I had to have it."

"Is that what you had with you in the garment bag?" Mama asked. "You'll have to model it for us later."

Hannah absently wiped down the last table and started putting placemats down. *If money's so tight and they're so worried, why did they spend money on a fancy pageant dress?* she wondered.

"Walt's going to steer wrestle," Hannah told Caylin after lunch. "He needs someone to watch his technique. You want to watch, too?"

"Sure." Caylin stood up from petting Hunter on the front porch.

The girls sat on the gate. Hannah had surprised herself by agreeing to watch, because just this morning, hearing Walt even mention the rodeo had made her angry. But she guessed she was tired already of sitting on the sidelines. Besides, she knew Caylin had never seen anything like this, and she wanted her friend to have a good time staying over.

"Has he found a way to practice his dismount off a horse?" Caylin asked. "And doesn't he need to practice on more than one steer?"

"He's working on finding a way, but right now he just needs to practice this part."

Walt jumped aside and grabbed the young steer's short horns as the animal tried to charge past him. He threw the weight of his own shoulders into a twist. His biceps bulged, and the tough beast sprawled on its back. Immediately, Walt jumped out of the way. The critter's four hooves flew into the air, and the steer scrambled to its feet.

"Hands are better weapons than horns, I guess," Hannah said. "Hey Walt," she called, "you're getting good!"

Walt looked surprised by the compliment. "Thanks."

"That steer must weigh twice as much as him," Caylin said.

"Probably," Hannah laughed. "Papa said if it were much bigger, Walt would have to leave him alone."

"Do they have girl steer wrestlers in the rodeo?" Caylin wondered.

"I don't know," Hannah said. "But it looks kind of fun—not fun like riding Ebony, but still fun—like a challenge."

"Doesn't look fun to me," Caylin said. "Uh-oh. You have that look on your face."

Hannah jumped down from the fence. "Looks fun to me," she grinned. Walt had just finished a second tackle. "Hey, Walt, I want to try it."

# Chapter Six

# Wrestling the World

Walt laughed. "You want to wrestle this steer? You're not strong enough."

"I'm as strong as lots of boys my age. Just let me try it once."

"You don't even know how."

"I've watched you a million of times," Hannah argued. Suddenly the steer represented the rodeo that said she was too young to compete. "Let me try," she insisted. "You know I'm tough for my size."

Walt shrugged. "I'm not your guardian, I guess. If you've watched me a million times, you better remember the secret is in the twist. If you don't do that, it won't work. Just don't blame me if you get hurt."

"I won't get hurt."

Caylin was still sitting on the fence. Hannah glared at the steer grimly and then ran at him from behind. He wasn't expecting her. She tackled his horns. She threw her weight and wiry strength into the maneuver she'd seen Walt use to flip the steer on his back.

But the steer only flexed his muscular neck to raise his head, stubborn as Hannah's. Hannah found herself being half carried, half dragged on the young steer's stubby horns across the pasture toward the lodge.

"Let go of his horns, Hannah!" yelled Walt.

"Let go! Let go!" Caylin shrieked.

Hannah didn't dare let go. What would the steer do to her with those sharp horns once she dropped off?

"Ar-r-r-r-uf-ff!" Hunter shot into the pasture. He had the steer's leg in an instant.

Hannah let go. She rolled along the rough pasture grass, a small rock skinning her knee.

Papa cleared the front steps in a single bound, followed by Mama and three guests carrying their coffee cups. Seconds later, they were all standing at the pasture fence. Papa ran towards the retreating steer, making sure the animal had really lost interest.

"I told you, Hannah," Walt said, "you have to twist the critter's neck. Why'd you even bother to try if you weren't gonna listen?"

"Leave me alone," Hannah said. "I could've done it if I'd have wanted to. It's just a dumb boy thing—jumping on a wild animal."

"Not dumb," Walt said. "And not wild. Just mad."

"Please, kids, the guests." Mama examined Hannah's knees. She helped Hannah up. As they went inside, Hannah could hear Walt talking outside to Papa.

"Hannah rassles a steer like she does everything else—her own way. She won't listen to anyone. I tried to tell her not to try it, then I tried to tell her how to do it. She didn't even listen to—"

Walt's words were lost as the door shut behind Hannah and her mother.

"Walt says he can take me home," Caylin said quietly an hour later as she came upstairs with the third ice pack for Hannah's bruised knees.

"Don't be silly. This is nothing. I want you to spend the night. I haven't even seen your pageant dress." Hannah nodded toward a long garment in a department-store bag, hanging on the closet door. "Please try it on." Hannah felt a little embarrassed to have Caylin see her failed attempt to tackle the steer, not to mention all the guests who had rushed outside when they heard the yelling.

"Look at these shoes!" Caylin exclaimed as she untied the bottom of the dress bag and a pair of old-fashioned, high-button shoes tumbled out.

"Wow," Hannah breathed.

"We found them at a thrift shop. Mom said they're probably just made to look like old shoes, but they're perfect."

"They sure are," Hannah said. "Let's go show Mama."

"Tonight's entertainment, maybe," Papa chuckled, as moments later Caylin sauntered down the stairs, followed by a sore-kneed Hannah. Caylin's ankle-length gingham dress topped with a broad-brimmed straw hat made her look like a Southern belle.

"I could use the practice, Mr. Parmenter," Caylin said.

Hannah smiled wryly. "And I've already been today's entertainment for the guests." *What a day,* she sighed to herself.

That evening Caylin did practice. Mama gathered Beaver Lodge's guests in front of the blazing fireplace, and Caylin sang for them—beautifully, even though there was no piano.

Hannah knew that Caylin was good enough to win Miss Lakeland, maybe even Mesquite Miss of Maine. But she couldn't stop thinking about the rodeo and what the officials might say when they called.

"Mama, can we call the rodeo now?" Hannah had found Mama in a guest room changing the bed for new guests. It was 12:05 p.m. on Monday, and Mama had promised to call again in the afternoon if the rodeo hadn't returned her call.

"Hannah." Mama's tone was between annoyance and amusement, and Hannah hoped she decided to be amused. Mama had not been pleased when Hannah wrestled the steer on Saturday, and Hannah didn't want to upset her mother again. But sometimes it seemed like no one understood how important being in the rodeo was.

Mama stuffed a pillow into its hunter green case. "It's barely noon," she said, pointing at the bedside alarm clock. "For goodness sake. It's still morning in Texas. We'll wait until three o'clock our time, and that might be pushing it. Until then, you have your biography of Hudson Taylor to read and the rest of your unit study on China to do. I'll come help you with it after lunch if you like."

"Yes, Mama," Hannah said. *Three whole hours!* She paused in the doorway. "And thank you, Mama."

"You're welcome," Mama said.

❋ ❋ ❋ ❋ ❋ ❋ ❋

Hannah was just reading how no one believed Hudson Taylor could ever be a missionary in China when the phone rang. She ran into the kitchen, but Mama had already answered it. Mama nodded at her, and Hannah listened anxiously to her end of the conversation. It was frustrating. Everything Mama said, she already knew.

Finally Mama hung up.

"Well?"

"Well, there's still hope," Mama said. She began rifling through a stack of papers by the telephone. "They said that rejected applications are destroyed. So there's no way they can read yours again and find your note."

"So I'm thrown out because of *their* stupid mistake?"

"Wait a minute. Let me finish. They asked us to send in a new one for the committee to review."

"But we don't have another application."

Mama held a paper up in triumph. "Yes we do." Her eyes twinkled. "For once my photocopying everything has paid off instead of just creating a lot of extra paper lying around."

"You mean?" Hannah thought she was beginning to understand.

"That's what I mean. Before you mailed the applications, I opened the envelope and made photocopies, then sealed the envelope with tape. It's good to prepare for mistakes and misunderstandings and lost mail." Mama nodded toward where a small photocopier sat on Papa's office desk.

"Can I go to Laketon and fax it now?" Hannah asked.

"If you come right back. We do need to work on

China. And Hannah," she cautioned, "this person couldn't promise what the committee would decide about the cutoff for turning thirteen. I suggest that as you watch this application go through Editor Farrington's fax machine, you put this into the Lord's hands and relax, okay? If you don't, it'll be a long week of waiting."

"I'll try, Mama. "

"Let's just proceed," Mama said. "Keep practicing. We'll trust the Lord to open this door."

Hannah nodded. "I'll try." She did feel like getting back on Ebony. Maybe, just maybe, they'd fly. Hannah grinned, remembering the flying, winged red horse on the gas station sign in Laketon.

# Chapter Seven

# New Boots and a Million Candles

"I'll get it!" Hannah cried, racing to catch the kitchen telephone. It was Saturday morning, a week since Caylin had come to the island to spend the night.

"Mama!" Hannah was practically shouting. "There's a fax at the *Gazette* office—it's for *me*. Editor Farrington needs me to pick it up right away. He stays only until noon on Saturday. There's only one reason I would be getting a fax."

"And we all know what that is," Mama chuckled. "Why don't you take the spare boat and go get it? I'll finish up breakfast here."

"Hey, if you're going to Laketon, take a look at the new cowboy boots in Fales' Outfitters," Walt called from the living room.

"Here's hoping I'll need them," Hannah called back. She took off her waitress's apron and ran upstairs to get some money. Of course she'd need the boots. The committee had to say yes. Hannah crammed a bunch of five- and one-dollar bills, tips from waiting on lodge guests that summer, into her wallet as she trotted to Beaver Island's boat dock.

It seemed like it took her forever to get to the *Gazette* office. She argued with herself the whole way, even as she walked into the office and stood at Editor Farrington's desk and waited for him to find the fax. *What if the committee says no? They can't say no. But what if they do?*

Finally, Editor Farrington found the letter in a stack of papers. "This fax came in last night, after we closed for the day. Know someone in Dallas?" he chuckled, noticing the return address.

*Just hurry up and give it to me,* Hannah felt like saying. Instead she took the fax calmly from him when he held it out. TEXAS MESQUITE RODEO ASSOCIATION, DALLAS, TEXAS was the name in bold letters across the top.

*Dear Ms. Hannah Parmenter:*

the letter began. Hannah felt her back break out in cold goose bumps.

*We have reviewed your reapplication. Since you will be thirteen before the rodeo opens, you may compete in the barrel race at the Skowhegan, Maine, State Fair Texas Mesquite Rodeo.*

*Please accept our apology for this mixup....*

Tears of joy rolled down Hannah's face as she turned to Editor Farrington. "Please let me use your phone," she gasped, crying and laughing all at once.

"Glad to!" He pointed to a phone on his desk.

"No one answers." Hannah dried her tears on her sleeve. She frowned, then grinned. "I'm in the rodeo!" She had to tell someone. A surprised Editor Farrington suddenly became the object of a bear hug.

Embarrassed, Hannah let the poor man go. "Mama must be outdoors. I gotta run tell Caylin—and my aunt and uncle. Hey, thanks!"

Hannah had raced down the street before Bill Farrington could tell her she owed him a dollar for the fax. "My contribution to the cause, I guess," he chuckled.

Moments later, Hannah and Caylin were surprised as they raced hand-in-hand across the Boudreaus' backyard to see Mama tying Beaver Lodge's big motor launch to the Laketon public dock.

"Hey, Mama!" Hannah waved the fax. "Why on earth did you follow me?"

Mama, panting, caught her breath from running up from the dock. Uncle Joe and Aunt Theresa rushed into the backyard. "Sandy, you're still wearing your apron—whatever is the matter, girls?" Aunt Theresa asked.

"May I see your fax, Hannah?"

"Sure, Mama."

"I guess I've got some kid in me yet," Mama laughed. "When Hannah got that call about a fax for her, we knew what it had to be—so I followed her here in our other boat as soon as my last guest finished breakfast. I couldn't wait, either. I wanted to be here when she found out what they'd decided."

"What's it about?" asked Uncle Joe.

"Hannah's in the rodeo!" Caylin squealed.

"Why, for mercy's sakes—we knew that all the time, Sandy!"

"You did, Auntie?" Hannah shot a puzzled glance at Aunt Theresa. Then she began to laugh. Quickly, she explained to her aunt and uncle about the mixup over her birthdate. She had decided not to tell them about her letter from the rodeo until she knew for sure she was out.

"No wonder you weren't over here talking rodeo with me," Uncle Joe said. "Well, I guess if I had started cleaning out the garage and you didn't get in, I would've had a clean garage out of the deal."

Caylin shot Hannah a surprised look.

"You didn't tell your Uncle Joe and Aunt Theresa?" Mama asked. "I guess I assumed you had. She hasn't created extra work for you, I hope?"

Uncle Joe shook his head. "No problem."

Hannah bit her lip. She hadn't thought about what would happen if Uncle Joe cleaned the garage and then Ebony didn't come.

Mama smiled. "Good. I've *got* to get back to the island before our guests miss me. Why don't you go shopping for those riding boots you wanted, Hannah. I'm sure Caylin would like to help you pick them out. Oh, Hannah?"

"Yes, Mama?"

"Don't let your heart run away with your head— okay? Spend your money wisely."

"I'll use my head, Mama."

Aunt Theresa shook her head as Mama hurried for the motor launch. "I'd say your mother's excited for you, dear."

"Yeah," Hannah laughed. She eyed her uncle. He didn't look mad, and she didn't see why he should be. There had been no harm done. He said he hadn't started to clean out the garage, but surely he still intended to.

"Do you want to come over later to practice, Caylin?" Aunt Theresa asked.

Caylin nodded. "That'd be great. Han, if you want me to go shopping with you, we should go now."

"Sure," Hannah said. "Talk to you guys later?"

"Later," Uncle Joe said. "We have a lot of work to do to get you and Ebony ready."

Hannah grinned. She knew she could count on Uncle Joe.

Fales' Outfitters had a pair of rubber boots just Hannah's size marked "Half Price—$10." Hannah bought them at once, remembering the Bean boots that were too small for her. She didn't want to wear her new riding boots for barn chores. Then Hannah asked to see the riding boots Walt had told her about.

"Usually I don't have much call for cowboy boots," Sam Fales chuckled. "But a Texas bootmaker went belly up, and he was selling his stock for fire-sale prices, so I ordered several dozen pair. Some of the better ones are rattlesnake skin—expensive stuff." Mr. Fales pointed to a large magazine ad he'd hung on the wall. "With the Texas Mesquite Rodeo coming to Maine, people been grabbing 'em up, so I figure I'll get my money out of 'em. You going?"

"I sure am!" laughed Hannah.

"She almost didn't," giggled Caylin.

"Let's see—ladies' size eight. Rattler skin—best there is." Sam Fales opened a shoe box from a pile in his display.

"Totally coo-ool!" Caylin said. "Gorgeous!"

"Oo-ooh!" said Hannah as she lifted the boots from the box. The red boots fit her perfectly, and they were the exact same boots as those in the big ad. "I like 'em!"

"I'm not sure they're you, Hannah," Caylin said, serious at last. "Too flashy."

Mr. Fales scowled, then forced a smile.

Hannah knew Caylin's taste in clothes was good. So she tried on three more pairs, two of which fitted poorly. "I need them to ride in the rodeo," she told Mr. Fales.

"You're *in* the rodeo? Well, you *are* growing up!"

Hannah fished the fax from her pocket and passed it to Mr. Fales. "Well, I'll be!"

"I...I think I'd like to try the snakeskin pair on again."

"Good choice, young lady." He glanced at the box, then turned it so Hannah could see "$180" penned on the end. "For a gal that's riding in the rodeo, I'll make a special price: a hundred and twenty."

Hannah caught her breath and glanced again at the ad on the wall. The ad said these boots had sold for six hundred, she noticed then. *Wow!* she thought. But Mr. Fales's price still surprised her. No one in her family had ever paid that much for shoes.

Hannah put on her sweetest smile and looked Mr. Fales right in the eye. "May I see those hand-tooled steerhide boots again, please?" She pointed to the only other pair that had fit her.

"Certainly." Mr. Fales sounded disappointed, but he forced a smile. The price marked on the box was eighty dollars.

Hannah slipped the boots on and walked to the mirror. These boots were beautiful, too, perhaps more so than the snakeskin boots. *But the snakeskin boots look so...so rich!* Hannah thought, eyeing them once more. She imagined herself riding in the rodeo wearing them. "Can...can I put the boots on layaway until next time I come to town? I've got more money at home."

"Sure, for a ten percent deposit, either pair. Or I can let you have the steerhide boots today for sixty dollars."

Caylin silently bit her lip.

Hannah thought for a moment. Ten percent of a hundred twenty was twelve. Or she could probably pay for the hand-tooled steerhide boots with the money she had with her. *But it's those beautiful rattlesnake-skin boots that I really want. It's my decision! Mama sent me to choose for myself. I have enough money to buy either pair.* Hannah's thoughts spun. *But I also promised her I'd be sensible. Double the price isn't very sensible. Not at all.*

"I'll be back in a little while when I decide, Mr. Fales," Hannah said at last, stepping out of the steerhide boots into her own shoes. "Thanks for your help."

Caylin followed Hannah out the door. "What are you going to do?" "Well," Hannah said, "I don't know. Or I think I do know. Did you like the steerhide ones?"

"I thought they looked good," Caylin said. "They looked more like you. When you were wearing those snakeskin ones, that's all I noticed—your boots. They were beautiful, but I can't picture you actually riding in them."

"Yeah?" Hannah said. She pictured Kennie MacKenzie racing and tried to imagine the red boots on her. She couldn't. "I think I'm going to go back and get those steerhide ones."

By the time Hannah got back to Beaver Island with her boots and her fax from the rodeo, Mama, Papa, and Walt were eating supper.

"Papa," Hannah cried, "you've got to see my fax." She presented it with a flourish over his plate of meatballs and mashed potatoes.

Papa grinned. "Wonderful. We've got two rodeo nuts in the house again. Mama's told me all about it."

"All of Laketon's probably heard about it by now," Walt said.

Hannah rolled her eyes. "They have not."

"Where were you all this time?" Mama asked. "I was just about to call Joe and Theresa and see if they'd seen you. Put your stuff down and sit down to eat."

Hannah was still holding the bag with her boots in it and a bunch of stuff she'd just checked out from the library. She sat down. "I've got to show you my boots." She pulled one out of the box and held it up.

"It took you this long to get boots?" Walt asked.

"Caylin and I looked around at Western clothes. And I went to the library to find more magazines and books and stuff on barrel racing." She put the boot away.

"They're nice," Mama said. "How much were they?"

"Sixty. On sale."

Papa nodded. "That's reasonable. Take some food. A person's got to eat. Can't just live on rodeo dreams."

Hannah laughed. "I forgot." She dished herself up some food.

Walt took a big bite of mashed potatoes. "I think I'll go look for some boots Monday."

"We were just talking with Walt about how he's going to manage to practice," Mama said.

"I gotta think of something."

"I wonder," Papa said, "if we could check around here to see if anyone has some animals they'd let you practice on."

"There's got to be someone," Hannah said. "Oh, Walt, before I forget, if you do go to Fales' Monday, I need you to pick up a hat I put on hold. I'll give you the money."

Papa raised his eyebrows. "Just how much money do you have?"

"Enough for the hat. It's felt—genuine Stetson. Has Uncle Joe called today?" Hannah was wondering whether he'd called to say anything about when he'd clean out his garage.

"No, he hasn't." Mama buttered herself a roll. "Walt, why don't you ask around town next week."

Walt nodded. "I know the Johnsons have steers and horses. Maybe Jeff's even entering—we could practice together."

"Caylin said Beth Johnson's going to be in the pageant," Hannah said. "I'm glad I'm in the rodeo instead. I'd rather have these boots than a fancy dress any day."

"It's a good thing everyone's not the same," Mama said.

"That's for sure," Papa said. "I've been thinking, Walt, pay close attention to your technique so you're in control, not the animal. We don't want you gored on its horns."

"Gross," Hannah said.

Mama quit chewing. "Does that happen?"

"Rarely," Papa said. "But it could happen."

"Don't worry," Walt said. "I'm not going to get hurt. Is it all right if I go to Laketon tomorrow?"

"You should watch some videos, too," Hannah said. "Uncle Joe has tons. The girl I'm watching, you should see her. I've got to get as good as her. She goes around the barrels just like that, so clean, so tight—oh!" Hannah cried. She had knocked over her glass of milk. "Sorry!"

"Hannah!" Walt cried, jumping up to avoid the puddle running toward him. "Pay attention!"

Hannah grabbed her shopping bag out of the way. "I said I'm sorry."

Walt scowled at her. "You're not the only one on this planet, you know."

Mama came back with a dishrag. "Get the worst with this. You can take care of the kitchen tonight, since Walt ended up helping me serve the guests."

"Yes, Mama." *Boy, you'd think I'd spilled the milk*

*on purpose.* But nothing was going to bother Hannah today. She was in the rodeo.

As she cleaned the kitchen, that's all she could think about. *In in in!* She was in the rodeo. Who cared if she spilled the milk? Who cared if she had to do the dishes?

When Hannah was finished, she wiped her hands on Mama's blue checkered towel and went over to look at her boots. As she tossed some extra papers from the box into Mama's wood-fired kitchen stove, she found a label from the snakeskin boots that had been dropped in the box by mistake. *WARNING:* the label advised. *These are fine dress quality footwear. Rough use may cause snakeskin to peel.*

"Thank You, Jesus," Hannah said under her breath, "for helping me not to make a foolish, expensive mistake." She fished one of the hand-tooled steerhide boots out of the box to appreciate its workmanship under the bright kitchen light. These boots were meant for riders—not watchers sitting on the sidelines—riders like Hannah. Hannah and Ebony were going to be champions. Like Kennie Mackenzie.

Hannah carried her boots and the stack of magazines and books she had gotten from the library up to her room and dumped them on her bed. Already on her bed was an issue of *Rodeo* magazine, with a white address label with her name on it. *Who would have done that?* Next to it was a cardboard tube that Hannah recognized as a poster holder. It, too, had a mailing label on it. Hannah pulled a plastic cap off one end of the tube and pulled out a thirty-inch-long poster of Kennie MacKenzie, the Wyoming State junior champion barrel racer, tearing along on her horse at the Mesquite Rodeo in

Dallas, Texas. Kennie was the one Hannah had watched over and over at Uncle Joe's.

Could Uncle Joe have done this? Did he get her her very own subscription? Hannah sat on her bed and opened the magazine. There on the inside cover, next to a girl racing a black horse, were the words:

*For my champion,*

*Love, Papa*

Still holding the magazine, Hannah crept to her window. The autumn moon rose orange and bright over the forest east of Moosehead Lake. Far, far down the big lake, beyond Mt. Kineo, Moosehead stretched toward Canada to the north. Hannah changed her gaze to peer at the lights of little Laketon. The village's only traffic light turned yellow, then red, then green. Beyond that light, Hannah knew, lay the road to Skowhegan, and beyond Skowhegan—which once had been her home—lay a vast world.

But for now the moon lit Hannah's room like a million candles.

Hannah was in the rodeo.

# Chapter Eight

# Runaway

"Uncle Joe and Aunt Theresa are buying me a membership in the Laketon Riding Club, Mama." Hannah's emerald eyes shone as she hung up the phone from talking with her uncle.

"But I thought their stables were full."

"Uncle Joe said most members keep their horses at home and just bring them there for practice. And he found out for sure that I can barrel race. They have a junior rodeo arena there, not just a track."

"And your uncle will board Ebony for you?" Mama asked.

"Yup. I'm keeping Ebony in Uncle Joe's garage—it's an old horse stable, really, you know—and he'll help me train him. Caylin and I are gonna help him clean all the junk and old furniture from one stall this Saturday. Then he'll patch the floor. It'll be ready by Tuesday, he thought."

"Your aunt and uncle are doing a lot for you," Mama observed.

Hannah nodded. "There's one more thing. And it's Auntie's idea. If I can stay over there most nights and do my schoolwork at their house, I can get a lot more riding time in at the club." Hannah's sentence ended like a question.

"That sounds reasonable," Mama agreed, "but it'll make more work for everyone else in the family, so let's wait to talk with Papa about it. Is there anything else we need to settle about this rodeo—any more logistics?"

Hannah hadn't been going to ask Mama right at the same time she asked to stay in Laketon, but she figured she had better lay all her ideas on the table now.

"Well, you know Uncle Joe said he'd talk to Papa about picking Ebony up where the twelve-mile trail meets the logging road. And I was thinking that I'd like to invite Caylin to ride the twelve miles with me."

"You'd be by yourselves deep in the woods." Mama clearly did not like this idea.

"I'm used to being in the woods," Hannah said.

"On Beaver Island," Mama agreed. "This is different. You're just twelve years old."

"Thirteen, Mama," Hannah corrected. "It rounds out to thirteen."

"So it does."

"Someone has to ride him around, Mama."

"Hannah, we'll talk about this with Papa, too. I'm thinking Walt should ride those miles."

"Walt? Because he's a boy?"

"How old is Walt, Hannah?" Mama eyed her daughter briefly.

"Fifteen."

"Almost sixteen. And he's been going into the forest alone for several years, cutting firewood. That's dangerous adult work."

"Since he was about my age!" Hannah protested.

"*With* adult supervision at first," Mama pointed out.

Walt wandered into the kitchen. "What are you guys talking about?"

"Just that you probably should ride Ebony on the trail," Mama said. "But we'll talk about it later with Papa. Now both of you get to work. I will not have this rodeo interfere with your schoolwork."

"That's what I was doing when I heard you guys arguing."

"Sorry we disturbed you," Mama said.

Though angry, Hannah knew when to quit. She followed Walt into the living room to begin her home-schooling lessons.

"What are you scowling at?" Walt asked as Hannah banged her books around. "Whoever rides him on the trail doesn't matter. He's gonna get to the rodeo, and that's what you want isn't it?"

Hannah didn't answer.

"Who just called?" Walt asked.

"Uncle Joe. He got me a membership at the riding club."

"Uncle Joe just bought you a membership, and you're mad about not riding Ebony on the trail? Get a grip, Han."

"This ol' hoss stall ain't been used for more'n half a century," Uncle Joe chuckled. He, Hannah, and Caylin were busy on Saturday morning moving boxes, carrying old furniture, and dragging out junk piled into the stall in the old stable-garage behind Uncle Joe's house. The stable had been built about a century ago for a driving horse and carriage. Papa and Mama had decided that Hannah could stay in Laketon and that Walt would ride Ebony on the twelve-mile trail. They would rent a horse trailer to go behind Uncle Joe's truck, and on Tuesday Ebony would swim across the channel. That was only three days away.

"What's this?" Caylin cried. The girls tugged at a contraption of black leather straps and brass buckles in a pile of old straw. "Oof!" They dragged it into the sunlight.

"Harness—fer hitchin' a hoss to a drivin' buggy or sleigh. I'd plumb fergot that was back there."

"Ebony's harness is light nylon webbing. I can put it on him by myself," Hannah said, remembering the harness used on Beaver Island whenever Ebony was being rigged out to pull a sleigh full of tourists for a trot on the lake ice in winter. "Oof," Hannah said again, hauling the heavy harness alongside Uncle Joe's truck. "I can see it's a harness, now I've got it out here. But I could never put it on a horse."

"I could," chuckled Uncle Joe. "She is heavy, *non?*"

"But what did folks without big muscles do when they wanted to harness a horse?" Caylin wondered. "They didn't have nylon harnesses then, did they?" Uncle Joe, both girls knew, though not a big man, was tough from years of working in the woods. Even an old knee injury from a falling tree while logging hardly slowed him down.

"See that hook?" Uncle Joe pointed to where a big steel hook was screwed into a beam above the horse stall. The girls peered up into the shadows. "That was for a rope and pulley. Someone who is not so rugged, they could pull ze harness over ze hoss easily with ropes."

"I guess we can't all be tough, like you," Hannah giggled. "Ebony's gonna love this stall," she added, noticing that it was now nearly clean. A few new boards, and it would be as good as new.

"Did Walt find a way to practice?" Uncle Joe asked.

"Yeah. He and Jeff Johnson are going to work together."

"Is he ready for ze big ride on Tuesday? Not too many hosses back in those woods anymore. Not like in the old days."

"Yeah, I guess. I wanted to ride Ebony myself and take Caylin along. I don't know what's to hurt." Hannah sighed. "I read in the paper last week about two girls who hiked the length of the Appalachian Trail, all the way from Georgia to Maine, more'n a thousand miles."

"Fun for you, maybe, Hannah." Caylin swatted a fly that buzzed at her from the old horse stall. "Me, I'd get eaten alive by bugs an' mosquitoes. Total grossness!" she added, brushing off the fly she'd killed.

"Not an outdoors girl, eh?" Uncle Joe chuckled. "I read about the hikers, too. Took 'em all summer." He glanced at Hannah with a gleam in his eye. "How old did the newspaper say they were?"

"Both college girls," Hannah admitted.

"See there?" Uncle Joe said. "When you're in college, you may hike the Appalachian Trail yourself. When you're Walt's age, you may *hike* not only the twelve-mile trail, but clear 'round ze lake, *non?*"

Caylin and Uncle Joe both had a good laugh. In spite of herself, Hannah began to laugh, too. She was still mad, but no matter how much she wanted to stay mad, Uncle Joe always managed to make her smile.

"That's the spirit," Uncle Joe said. "If you're staying at my house this week, I want to see more of that smile."

"Can we show her the surprise now?" Caylin asked.

"Sure," Uncle Joe said, smiling. "Lead the way."

Hannah looked from Caylin to Uncle Joe. "Surprise?"

Neither of them said a word. Hannah followed them through the gate into the Coulsons' side yard. They stopped in front of a horse trailer. Why would the Coulsons get a horse trailer? They didn't even have a horse.

Caylin and Uncle Joe were watching Hannah expectantly.

"You got a horse trailer?" Hannah asked.

Caylin and Uncle Joe laughed.

"Uncle Joe bought it for Ebony, silly," Caylin said. "It's just here so we could surprise you."

"Oh, Uncle Joe, now we don't have to rent a trailer!" Hannah hugged Uncle Joe.

"Found this trailer down near Portland, and I told your Papa not to bother. Used, but it's in good shape. Figured with everybody gittin' into ridin' hosses 'round here, I could sell her after the fair an' make a few bucks, *non?*"

"You've always got a trade going, haven't you, Uncle Joe?" Hannah laughed.

"Give him all the rein, Hannah!" Papa let the canoe drift for a moment, then dipped his paddle and pulled until the reins with which Hannah led Ebony tightened.

Hannah peered into the water. The lake bottom here pitched off into the deep channel, down, down to where patches of water weeds poked up from the inky blackness. "Easy, boy," Hannah cried to Ebony, who was up to his belly now. "You've been here before—remember?"

Ebony stepped to the edge of the channel. Suddenly he lost his footing and plunged in over his head.

"Tighten it, honey—draw in the slack! Quick! He'll try to head back to the island if you let him!"

Hannah pulled. Ebony surfaced, snorting and blowing. As Papa had said, as soon as Ebony got his bearings, he tried to turn back. Beaver Island was his home.

"C'mon, boy!" Hannah whooped. "You'n me are going to the rodeo." She was surprised at how nicely Ebony swam right along behind them. Papa kept the canoe moving steadily toward where Walt, with the saddle in the motorboat, was already waiting at the point by Mr. Morris's cabin. They would call Uncle Joe as soon as they got back to let him know that Walt had started out.

Ebony soon found his footing in the shallow water beyond the channel. Suddenly he bolted, turning back toward Beaver Island.

Hannah yanked the reins tight. The canoe rolled over. Hannah floundered in waist-deep water, fighting Ebony for control.

Papa lunged for the reins as they tore from Hannah's hands, but before he could really grip them, Ebony had bucked and wheeled. Free, he plunged back into the channel and swam for Beaver Island. Papa swam after him, reaching for the floating reins.

Hannah began to swim after Papa.

"Go back, Han!" Papa hollered. He turned midchannel and swam back toward Hannah. "We might as well try to catch a freight train."

"Whatever got into him, anyway, Papa?" Hannah

was in tears as she and Papa hauled the partly submerged canoe toward the point.

"Homing instinct—all animals have it, more or less. Walt!" Papa motioned to Walt.

Walt was already hurrying out to them with the motorboat. He cut his motor. "What should I do, Papa?"

"Go see if you can catch Ebony on this side of the island while we empty the water out of this canoe."

Walt shot away. He roared back to the point with the motorboat just as Hannah and Papa got the canoe to float again. "No sign of Ebony!"

"Horse got it in his head it's time to head for home." Papa gave Hannah a wet squeeze around the shoulders. Both of them were soaked. "Don't worry, Han. We'll find him in the pasture with Molly, I reckon." He helped Hannah into the canoe.

"But, Papa, what'll I do?"

"We'll try again."

"This afternoon?"

"I wish I could, but I've got guests to entertain this afternoon. I'll do it as soon as I can, honey, but I do have other responsibilities."

"Tomorrow morning then?"

Papa held her gaze. "I said I'd try. It might be several days before I can take time off again. I already rescheduled things today. You know I have tour groups to guide and chores at the lodge."

"Well, we're not going to get good practicing in our pasture." Hannah fought tears and grabbed her paddle. Didn't Papa understand? "You don't know how important this is," she blurted out. "You don't even care."

Papa stopped mid-stroke, his paddle hanging into the water. "Hannah, I wouldn't be here right now if I didn't care." He started to paddle again, and Hannah looked away from his brown eyes probing hers from under his bushy eyebrows. "What do you want me to do? Send all the tourists home? Should I say, 'I know this is the first vacation you've had in years, and I know you flew here all the way from Kansas, but I can't guide you on your wilderness adventure after all'? Hannah, we do have bills to pay."

Hannah stared into the dark water.

"You know," Papa said softly, "we have to consider whether an animal with that much homing instinct can even be made to go to Laketon. I'll see what Uncle Joe knows. He's expecting our call anyway."

Hot tears slid down Hannah's freckled cheeks. Nobody understood how important winning the barrel race was.

"And Hannah," Papa said when Hannah didn't answer, "I expect you to understand that I'm doing my best."

Dip-and-push, dip-and-push, dip-and-push. Hannah paddled for Beaver Island, biting her lip until she tasted blood.

# Chapter Nine

# "Ride 'em, Cowgirl!"

Hannah sat sadly in the corner of Papa's office that evening as Papa phoned Uncle Joe in Laketon. "You sure you can manage him, Joe?" Hannah's hopes soared, sank, soared again as she heard Papa talking with Uncle Joe.

"I'll let you talk with her." Papa passed Hannah the phone.

"Yes, Uncle Joe? Oh, you will! Wow! Tomorrow? Cool, thanks! Bye."

"MAMA...WALT!"

Mama and Walt hurried into Papa's office to hear what was up.

"Uncle Joe'll help me bring Ebony across the channel tomorrow morning—if we can use Papa's rowboat instead of the canoe."

"Good idea," Papa agreed. "Ebony can't tip the rowboat over so easily. I'm taking a party of guests fishing over in Spencer Bay, so I'll be busy all day."

"I was gonna fix the fence tomorrow," Walt said, "but I guess I can do that Thursday."

"Only," Mama murmured, thinking. "Only someone needs to meet you with Uncle Joe's pickup at
the end of the logging company's road."

"Did he say anything to you about that, Papa?"
Hannah asked.

"No problem," Papa said. "Joe will head right
back to Laketon after Walt's on his way. He'll have
time to drive around."

Hannah grinned. Everything was set. That night
she lay across her bed in her pajamas, propped up
on her elbows, flipping through her *Rodeo* magazine. Her stomach was jittery. All she could think
about was riding Ebony under the lights at the fair's
arena. For what had to be the tenth time, she
flipped to an interview with Kennie MacKenzie. The
article had a picture of her riding full speed through
a barrel course on her painted mustang. Her red felt
Stetson was tied under her chin, and her dark hair
flew out behind her, just above her shoulders. Her
red and white Western shirt was a blur, and her
jean-clad legs ended in boots in her stirrups.

Hannah imagined Kennie's knees guiding her
horse as she had seen her do on Uncle Joe's rodeo
tape. The interview said Kennie was fifteen. She was
the junior champion barrel racer for the whole state
of Wyoming. In the interview, she talked about how
her favorite horse had broken a leg. She had to start
over, then spend another year training before she
won her state's championship. Her next big event
was the Texas Mesquite Rodeo in Dallas, and she
was the favorite to win.

Hannah stared at the long poster of Kennie on
her closet door. It showed her tearing along on her
horse, probably in one of her winning races. Hannah
pulled down her comforter and crawled under the

covers. Willing herself to sleep, she switched her lamp off and stared at the shadows on her ceiling. What would it be like to win? Would Kennie come to Maine to compete? In the interview she said she home schooled because she followed the rodeo circuit several months of the year. 15.3—that was the time Hannah needed to match Kennie's Wyoming championship time.

A soft rap came at the door. "May I come in?" It was Mama.

"Yes?" The lighted dial on Hannah's clock radio said 11:00.

Mama sat on the edge of Hannah's bed. "I just saw your light turn off."

Hannah propped herself up on one elbow. Was something wrong? No, in the moonlight it looked like Mama was smiling.

"Just wanted to say goodnight. I realized you'll turn thirteen while you're in Laketon."

"I'll see you before then, Mama."

Mama brushed her fingers through Hannah's tangled curls. "Yes, I guess you will."

Hannah settled back down on her pillow. "Will you come watch me and Ebony practice at the club?"

"I wouldn't miss it. Now get some sleep. I could use some help in the morning before Joe comes. We've got a lot of guests registered to come this week."

"Sure, Mama."

Mama moved from the moonlight's reach into a shadow. Softly, she closed the door behind her.

Hannah smiled and pulled the covers tighter around her. Tomorrow, Ebony would be in Laketon, and Thursday, they would be at the Laketon Riding Club.

Finally.

❋ ❋ ❋ ❋ ❋ ❋ ❋

"Ride 'em cowgirl! Ride that bronco!" hollered Uncle Joe from his perch on the fender of his pickup truck at the Laketon Riding Club. Getting Ebony across the channel Wednesday had been uneventful—the only easy thing that had happened since Hannah had decided to enter the rodeo.

The club was perfect. The stables and arena and track were backed by woods laced with riding trails, and the whole place was surrounded by tall pines.

"Yeee-haah!" Hannah hollered. "Go, boy!" She slapped the base of Ebony's neck with her Stetson hat and dug her knees into his ribs. Leaning low, holding back his power, shortening his stride, Ebony galloped around a yellow plastic barrel Uncle Joe had found at a factory in Skowhegan, then drove himself powerfully across to the second.

"Stride long, Ebony, c'mon," Hannah yelled. She leaned deep to the left with Ebony. "Long, I said long!" Ebony's steps were too short. He still hadn't found the right rhythm. Horse and rider looped wide around barrel two. Barrel three seemed better.

"How's my time?" Hannah asked anxiously as she trotted the big stallion up to the fence.

"Good for us, but still over eighteen seconds—he's still taking too many little steps around the barrels. And you just lost points."

"What did I do this time?"

"Ze third barrel. It jiggled as you went past. That's a no-no, *non?*"

"I'll *never* be any good." Hannah slapped Ebony with her Stetson again, and he began to pace nervously.

"Hold your hosses, young lady," Uncle Joe warned. "Ebony's had a big week. Don't forget that you've got the best trainer north of Texas and one of ze best hosses around." Joe Boudreau's knowledge of horses was a legend across the state of Maine— at least among those who also worked with horses.

"Then why can't we seem to get it? We've been practicing for weeks at home, and he still hits the stupid barrels or tiptoes around them! Don't you know anything that will help us?"

"Last week I read in ze newspaper that ze city of Rome really *was* built in a day," Uncle Joe joked.

Hannah scowled. "What's *that* supposed to mean? That's *not* funny!" Was helping her and Ebony get ready for the rodeo as hopeless as building a whole city in a day?

"Why don't you just take a time-out? We've been here several hours already. Remember, this is only your second day at the club."

"I don't want to take a time-out. We have work to do. I say Ebony kicks barrels, you say take a break—breaks are not gonna make us better. You're supposed to help make us better."

Uncle Joe looked at her quietly, then slid down from the fender of his pickup. "Perhaps you'd like to practice alone," he said. "I've got things to do." He opened his truck door and got in.

Just like that. Hannah watched Uncle Joe's truck disappear around the bend toward the village of Laketon. She was sorry Uncle Joe got his feelings hurt, but did he have to leave? Usually he had a sense of humor. Hannah guided Ebony to the starting line she had toed in the dirt, the proper distance from the first barrel. She would just have to practice with Ebony alone, if that's how Uncle Joe felt.

Ebony was galloping full speed down the arena to the third barrel when Hannah spotted Caylin

walking across the gravel parking lot. Hannah finished the course and trotted over to meet her.

"Aunt Theresa said you were still down here,"
Caylin said. "I thought you'd be back for supper by
now."

Hannah groaned and looked at her watch.
"Supper. I forgot. Now Auntie will be mad at me,
too."

Caylin looked puzzled. "She had a place set for
you, but she didn't seem mad or anything."

"Good." Hannah didn't feel like talking about
Uncle Joe just yet. "I thought you'd come after
school. Where were you?"

"Where were *you* yesterday? You never called to
tell me you weren't coming. And today, my mom
actually *made* me take a nap after school." Caylin
laughed. "Can you believe it? Since I haven't been
feeling very good, she said I should."

"I was pretty busy trying to figure out how I'd get
Ebony here," Hannah said. "Hey, I'd better head
back. You want to ride with me?"

"Sure."

Hannah scooted forward and took her foot from
the stirrup so Caylin could use it to swing from the
fence onto Ebony's back behind her. The girls rode
out of the club gate and along the road's wide
shoulder. It was only a mile to their street.

"How come Uncle Joe isn't here?"

"He...he got kind of upset and left," Hannah
said. "We didn't agree about how to train Ebony."

"Uncle Joe got mad?"

"Well, not mad. I don't know. He must have been
in a bad mood."

"That's funny."

Hannah was still explaining how she remembered her argument with Uncle Joe when she

stopped Ebony in front of Caylin's house. "Comin' to watch me practice tomorrow?"

"Come watch *me* practice?" Caylin said. "Aunt Theresa said tomorrow afternoon would be a good time for us to practice my pageant song. My mom and dad will be in Skowhegan all day."

"Oh. Well, I'll probably be at the club. But I'll see you later."

"Later," Caylin echoed.

Hannah hurriedly took care of Ebony and ran in the Boudreaus' kitchen door. "Sorry I'm late."

"There you are," Aunt Theresa said. "Wash up. Supper's ready."

Hannah washed her hands at the kitchen sink.

"Joe," Aunt Theresa called. "Hannah's here."

Would Uncle Joe be mad?

Uncle Joe came into the kitchen. "Hi, Hannah."

Hannah's eyes met his. "Hi." He seemed okay.

They all took their seats. Hannah waited through the prayer, the dishing up of food, and Aunt Theresa's story about an old friend who had called her today. The friend had just come back from a trip to a Romanian orphanage. "How much we here in America take for granted, like the love we've always had from our families!" Aunt Theresa said.

"Makes a person think, doesn't it?" Uncle Joe said.

"Sure does," Aunt Theresa said. "Oh, I almost forgot. I talked to your mom today, Hannah. They have a lot of guests, just about a record for this time of year. Can you believe it? But it sounds like everything's going well. Even Walt's got a sense of humor about doing your chores—said he feels a bit like the older brother of the prodigal son story staying home doing all the work."

"Very funny," Hannah said.

Hannah saw Uncle Joe and Aunt Theresa exchange a glance.

"Your family sure wants you to have a good shot at this rodeo," Aunt Theresa said.

"Yeah," Hannah said.

Uncle Joe took another piece of ham. "You know, Hannah, I've been thinking since I came home."

Hannah waited. Was he going to apologize for leaving?

"You can't let yourself get discouraged," Uncle Joe said. "Think about it. When you're frustrated, you can't concentrate on your techniques, so instead of getting better, your race stays the same or gets worse—the very opposite of what you want."

Hannah played with her mashed potatoes. This didn't sound like an apology.

"Don't lose perspective, Hannah, or life will get lost in the race, and you'll lose the race, too. Keep your attitude positive, and let Jesus take care of the important things."

"You make it sound easy," Hannah sighed.

"It isn't," Uncle Joe admitted. "But it's easier than a life of frustration."

"Uncle Joe, maybe Ebony just isn't the right horse," Hannah said. "Do you think an Arabian stallion could win this kind of rodeo event? Mustangs and quarter horses are supposed to be cowboy horses."

"True," Uncle Joe agreed. "But we'll give it our best shot. Be diligent. I can't promise you Ebony will win, but he'll certainly improve. Think of how far you guys have already come."

"Pie, Hannah? Joe?" Aunt Theresa got up and poured herself and Uncle Joe some coffee. "It's raspberry."

"Sure," Hannah said. Raspberry was her favorite.

"Thanks," said Uncle Joe.

"Tomorrow's a new day, eh?" Uncle Joe said.

Hannah smiled. "Yeah." As she ate Aunt Theresa's delicious pie, things did seem to look brighter.

One morning when Hannah came down for breakfast, she found Uncle Joe chatting in French on his CB radio. "That was my old friend, Gilbert Daigle," he said to Hannah, signing off. "I think he can help you, mebbe."

"Oh? How?" Hannah sat down at the table next to Uncle Joe.

"I've been thinking about how Ebony's been taking so many little steps around the barrels. Gil will be down from the woods this afternoon. I asked him to meet us at the club today to look at Ebony's feet."

Hannah laughed. "Ebony's feet? You always have something funny planned."

A smile played on Uncle Joe's lips and in his eyes.

"What *do* you have planned?" Hannah asked.

"Don't you trust me?"

"Well, Ebony is my horse. And it is my race."

"I understand," Uncle Joe said. "You trust my good intentions, but not necessarily my plan. Well, here's my idea. We take his heavy steel shoes off and replace them with light aluminum ones. That should help him take longer, smoother steps around the barrels—and save you time."

"Oh, Uncle Joe, we could win. He'd—" Hannah stopped. "How do you know it'll work? Have you tried it before?"

"It's been done, but there's no guarantee. The

key will be whether Ebony keeps tight around the barrels or goes wide. If he goes wide, you lose time. It's the risk you take."

"Well, Ebony's probably not going to win the way he's stepping through the turns now," Hannah said. "It's the tiny fractions of a second that make the big difference."

"True," Uncle Joe said.

Hannah sighed. "And then if he tips even one barrel, we get docked more time. I mean lots of times he does it perfectly, but I can't count on it. If it were your race, Uncle Joe, would you do it?"

"I would. But the decision is yours."

Hannah thought for a moment. It might make Ebony slower, or it might not do anything—or it might help him win. "I'll do it," she said.

"Gonna race this horse, miss?" Gil Daigle asked.

Hannah watched as Mr. Gilbert Daigle, a traveling horse farrier and blacksmith, carefully trimmed each of Ebony's hooves. Mr. Daigle had removed each of Ebony's four heavy steel shoes. Now he nailed light aluminum ones in their place.

"Well, sorta," Hannah answered. "We're in the Texas Mesquite Rodeo—the barrel race—at Skowhegan State Fair."

"Aluminum shoes are for track racing. Most rodeo riders use reg'lar steel shoes." Mr. Daigle shook his head, puzzled. "But that's what your Uncle Joe asked for. And he's the best horseman around!"

"*Merci, merci beaucoup*, Gil," chuckled Uncle Joe as he paid Mr. Daigle. "Thanks for the compliment. You want another twenty dollars for that?" Uncle

Joe winked at Hannah. Then seriously, he added, "Now we're gonna teach ze pig to fly!"

"Pigs certainly *can't* fly!" Hannah exclaimed as she and Ebony tried again and again to find the right rhythm around the barrels. Ebony's steps were longer, but each time through, either they gave up too much speed or Ebony tipped a barrel, and a couple of times he even sent one rolling across the arena. This was the worst day of practice Hannah had had since bringing Ebony to the mainland from Beaver Island.

"He's *faster*, Hannah!" Caylin had come over after school to help out. She held up the new stopwatch Hannah had bought. "Almost down to seventeen seconds."

"Yeah, but he still doesn't have a consistent rhythm!"

"I expected that at first," Uncle Joe said. "Give him time to get used to his new shoes."

Hannah stroked Ebony's neck. "How do we know this'll work?"

"We don't, of course," Uncle Joe said. "Remember, I told you that."

"Yeah," Hannah sighed. "I guess you did." She gritted her teeth. "We're gonna teach *this* pig to fly, yet. Hup, big feller! Yahoo!" She slapped her hat and set Ebony at a gallop again. She sure hoped Uncle Joe's idea wasn't crazy.

# Chapter Ten

# Hannah the Spy

"Well," chuckled Aunt Theresa one afternoon as Hannah and Uncle Joe returned from practice, "the lawn at the Shozenski place is getting mowed *twice* this season."

"They're back?" Hannah asked. "I've never even met the Shozenskis. Oh, hi, Caylin."

"Hi. Hey, you guys should have heard Aunt Theresa playing the piano today—she's getting good."

Aunt Theresa blushed. "You're the star. I'm just your accompaniment." She opened the door to the back porch. They could hear the "Br-r-r-rp, ar-room! Br-r-r-rp, ar-room!" of a power mower being rammed into too-tall grass and yanked back again and again. "They're over there right now. Their girl is cutting the yard."

"Oh? What's her name?" Hannah wondered.

"Serena. I kin hear Mrs. Shozenski yelling her name once in a while," Uncle Joe said. "They're a noisy bunch, that crowd. Sometimes has parties on their terrace by the lake, and you kin hear music and kids yelling till real late."

"No wonder the mother yells," Aunt Theresa said, "with those radio headphones the girl's always wearing."

"I seem to remember a certain girl from Skowhegan," Uncle Joe teased. "She used to play her 45 RPM records so loud the neighbors complained."

"Who, me?" Aunt Theresa laughed.

"Maybe her mother could get a walkie-talkie tuned to the same channel as her radio," Hannah snickered, remembering the walkie-talkies they used on Beaver Island.

"Actually," Caylin said, "Serena's pretty cool. It's just that for them Laketon is a vacation place. They figure Laketon is the end of the world, and they can make all the noise they want."

"So where do the Shozenskis think the real world is?" Hannah asked.

"Noo Yawk," Caylin imitated. "Serena can see the New York City skyline across the Hudson River from her home in New Jersey. She told me she'd love to live there."

"Well, I wouldn't!" said Hannah, who remembered her trip with Papa and Mama to Manhattan in downtown New York. "All those skyscrapers—you feel like you're living in a deep box!"

"Well Serena likes it. She talks about it a lot."

"Sounds like you're friends," Aunt Theresa said.

Caylin shrugged. "Since they're the next house behind ours on the waterfront, I've done some stuff with her."

"Caylin should introduce you, Hannah," Aunt Theresa suggested. "Since coming over from the island, all you've seen is a horse and..."

"And old folks," chuckled Uncle Joe.

"Well, there's you, Caylin," Hannah laughed.

"And I've seen practically nothing of you, you've

been so busy with Ebony. You like horses better than people lately." Caylin wrinkled her nose.

"I do not. I have too seen you."

"Well, c'mon. I'll introduce you." Caylin's red curls bounced as she stood up.

Hannah and Caylin cut through Caylin's yard and out onto the street in front of the Shozenski place. A tall girl wearing cut-off shorts was pushing an old gas mower up a slope in the front yard. She had writing all over her T-shirt, Hannah noticed.

The girl spotted them on her way back down. "Hi, Caylin," she shouted. She stopped the mower in front of them and let it idle noisily. Now Hannah could see that the writing on her shirt was signatures. On the front of the white T-shirt "Franklin Junior High" was silk-screened in red block letters.

"Hi," Caylin said. "Serena, this is Hannah; Hannah, Serena."

"Hi," Hannah said.

Serena smiled. "Hi." She tucked her blonde hair behind her ear. Hannah noticed her two silver stud earrings.

"So where do you live?" Serena asked. "I don't remember ever seeing you in town."

Hannah motioned toward the lake. "Beaver Island, just a couple minutes' boat ride."

"Her parents run a tourist lodge," Caylin offered.

"Wow, that must be even more of a wilderness vacation than this is," Serena laughed. "My friends couldn't believe it when I told them Laketon has only one stoplight."

"Laketon's tiny compared to where I used to live in Connecticut," Caylin agreed.

"But there you didn't have the lake," Hannah countered.

"True," Caylin said.

Serena was drumming her fingers on the mower handle. She had three silver rings on her left hand and three on her right. "Hey, Caylin, remember that party we had on my dock this summer? We should invite everyone again."

Caylin glanced at Hannah. "Yeah, we should."

Hannah frowned. She hadn't heard about any dock party this summer.

"And remember that hike we went on? I have a picture of you next to the creek." Serena motioned at the house. "It's inside."

Hannah traced a crack in the sidewalk with the toe of her sneaker. "So, wanna come see my horse?" she asked.

"So you're the one with the horse? I saw you riding down the street this morning. Is he safe?"

"Safe?" Hannah was puzzled. "Well...sure."

"I mean, like, he doesn't kick or bite or anything?"

"No." Hannah giggled. This was funny. How could anyone think Ebony would be dangerous?

Serena shut her lawn mower off. "Hey, Mom!" she yelled without going inside, "a local wants me t' see her horse."

*Local.* Hannah wrinkled her nose, but she didn't say anything. *Why doesn't she just say girl?*

"Doing anything the rest of the day?" Caylin asked as they walked back to the Boudreaus.

Serena shrugged. "Not much. Unless you count picking up old bottles and cans tossed into our yard and cutting the grass."

"I guess it's rough when your house is closed up most of the year," Hannah said. "Some people use your yard for a dump."

"That's the breaks, I guess. Some of the locals are real creeps."

Hannah knew Serena was right. A few people

around Laketon did resent summer visitors. But the way Serena said *locals* made Hannah feel like she thought they were all creeps.

Hannah led Ebony from his stall.

"Cool," Serena said. "He's so-oo big. My mom would have a fit if she saw me riding past on him!"

"He's gentle," Caylin said. "See." She scrambled onto the body of Uncle Joe's truck, then slid on bareback. "I've gotten to ride him all over Hannah's island. It almost makes me wish *I* was gonna be in the rodeo."

"You're going to be in a rodeo, Hannah? For real? Oh, he's beautiful. Can I sit on him?—a real rodeo horse!"

"Sure," said Hannah. "Watch those beams, though." She pointed to where petite Caylin had bent over to keep her head from striking a large ceiling beam.

Caylin slid back down onto Uncle Joe's truck. Serena climbed onto the edge of the truck's bed, then onto the horse. "AAHH-CHOO!!" she sneezed, as dust from the old stable tickled her nose.

Ebony stepped around nervously.

"Easy, boy!" Hannah pulled his head down by the halter rope.

"OUCH!" Serena cried, cracking her head on a beam.

"Bend down and don't holler," Hannah said quietly, quickly, firmly.

Serena slouched down, clutching Ebony's mane in panic. "I can't get off," she whispered. Her brown eyes were wide. Ebony had sidled away from the truck. There was no way off the tall stallion without jumping to the floor, and Serena was obviously too scared to do that.

"Hang on!" Caylin said.

Ebony pranced around even more.

Hannah put a finger over her lips. "The saw-horse." She pointed to a wooden sawhorse next to her uncle's workbench. "Please get it, Caylin. Easy, Ebony; easy, boy."

Ebony settled down.

Caylin brought the sawhorse. Shaking, Serena slid onto it.

"That beast is crazy!"

"Just spooked," Hannah said. "Sorry." She led Ebony to his stall. When she returned, Caylin was examining a bruise on Serena's head. The roots of Serena's blonde hair were dark, Hannah noticed.

"You're fine" Caylin said. "Didn't even break the skin. You may get a lump, though."

"It felt like I left my scalp up there." Serena cast a wary look at the rough beams of the old stable, then wiped a tear from her face with the back of her hand. "Uh, I'll see you guys later, okay? I really promised my dad I'd finish mowing today."

"Sure," Caylin said, following Serena outside.

"Sorry about Ebony," Hannah said. She knew she had to say something.

"Guess I'd cry too if I'd never been on a horse before and he jumped so I cracked my head," Caylin said as soon as Serena was out of earshot.

"Guess so. But I wish she'd quit calling us *locals*. If she thinks it's so boring here, why doesn't she go back to New Jersey?"

"Duh, Hannah. She can't. Her parents are here. And she told me this summer that it's okay here. It's just that all her friends are at home. She's nice once you get to know her."

"Okay, I guess. I just met her," Hannah admitted. Caylin seemed to be awfully defensive. "She really went on a hike with you? Wasn't she afraid of bears or something?"

Caylin shrugged. "Maybe she was, but she went anyway."

"I haven't seen the Shozenski girl around at all. I guess with your horse and books, you're pretty busy." Aunt Theresa carefully measured vanilla into the frosting she was making. Hannah was going to bring several cakes home for the lodge guests in the morning.

"Serena's all right, I suppose." Hannah tapped her pencil against her grammar book, searching for words to describe the blonde vacationer two doors over. She had seen Serena only once since Caylin had introduced them. She spent all her time with Ebony. Caylin had said that Hannah should have her birthday party in Laketon, and Hannah and Aunt Theresa had agreed. Then Caylin said she should invite Serena, but Hannah hadn't decided yet. "It's just that she's...she's different. And..."

"We're all 'different,'" Aunt Theresa said.

*Uh-oh.* Hannah suddenly remembered something Mama had said about God's making us all individuals. Now she was gonna catch it from Aunt Theresa.

But Aunt Theresa changed the subject. "I never found out why Serena isn't in school. Do they start late in New Jersey?"

"They're building a new junior high school. It wasn't ready on time."

"Oh? They'll need to keep school into next summer, I guess. Poor girl! She must be lonely without her friends."

"Yes, I'm sure she's lonely." Hannah sighed again, remembering how Serena called everybody in Laketon "locals." It seemed rude to Hannah, even if Caylin said Serena didn't mean to be.

Aunt Theresa wiped a powdered-sugared hand on her apron. "Why don't you run right over and invite her to supper?"

"How do you invite someone to supper who doesn't eat supper?" The silly question flitted on butterfly wings through Hannah's brain—and out of her mouth. Folks from the New York City area, she knew from listening to tourists at Beaver Lodge, call dinner "lunch" and supper "dinner."

"Hannah," Aunt Theresa laughed, "if you think about your lodge guests, you'll remember that most of them are nice folks, wherever they're from—and whatever they call their evening meal."

"I know," Hannah said, putting her schoolbooks and papers in a neat pile on the kitchen table. "I'll go ask her." *At least the guests at the lodge want to be in Laketon,* Hannah thought. *What if she doesn't want to eat with me?*

For some reason Hannah found herself ducking into the bathroom on her way out the door. In the mirror was someone who looked—well, who looked like she had been racing a horse all morning and studying all afternoon. Hannah stuck her tongue out at herself, tucked some loose strands back into her French braid, and hurried outside.

It was a longer walk by way of the street, so Hannah cut through the gate in the backyard fence into the Coulsons' garden behind their garage. A thick row of scratchy blue spruces separated the Coulsons' backyard from the Shozenski side yard. Hannah squirmed through. The Shozenski household was deathly silent. *Maybe they've gone out.* But their big old station wagon with New Jersey plates was in the drive. *No, they're home, all right.*

Then Hannah saw Serena. Really, she heard her first. Serena was singing—loudly—off-key. She lay on a purple-striped cushioned chaise lounge in the backyard, holding a bottle of nail polish in one hand and the brush in the other. Serena wore headphones attached by a wire to a compact disk player on the ground. She waved her feet in time to a tune only she could hear, apparently to dry her toenails.

Hannah stopped. *Weird,* she decided. *Black toenails!* Wasn't Serena cold just sitting out here? It was sunny but hardly sunbathing weather.

Serena placed one foot carefully on the ground. Hannah cleared her throat. Then Hannah saw it: A rose tattoo decorated Serena's thigh, just below her khaki shorts.

Serena yanked her headset off and pushed her sunglasses up. "Spy!" she hissed. Serena glared at Hannah. "What are you doing sneaking around?"

"I did *not* sneak!'

"Our *guests* use the front walk."

"Serena, I.... "

"I could have you arrested for trespassing!"

Hannah smiled, imagining Sheriff Sylvester coming to put handcuffs on her for doing what kids all over Laketon did—cut across a backyard. "Serena, don't be ridiculous."

Serena jammed the nail polish brush into the bottle and stood up. In her hurry, she knocked her soda can over with her foot. "Rats!" She stooped to pick it up, then straightened and glared at Hannah. "What are you staring at?"

Hannah felt herself blushing. "Nothing." What she was staring at were the tattoos revealed by Serena's white tank top—one on each shoulder: a butterfly and a parakeet.

Serena's angry look mellowed into one of satisfaction. "Never seen a tattoo?"

"I have, too! What a...a jerk!" Hannah sputtered. "You think you're soo-o coo-ol 'cause you're from Noo Joisey! We're only dumb 'locals.' Well let me tell you something. You're no better'n us." Hannah ducked into the hedge of spruce trees. Their sharp needles tore at her arms and cheeks as she wriggled through them and ran for Aunt Theresa's house.

# Chapter Eleven

# A Crummy Party

"What do I do now, Mama? Serena lives practically next door to Aunt Theresa's. I almost have to invite her." Hannah had decided to go home to Beaver Island right after dinner instead of in the morning. She couldn't believe it. She had gone over to the Shozenskis to make a friend—at least Aunt Theresa had wanted her to make a friend—and she had left with an enemy. Or maybe she could believe it. She had known right away what Serena thought of *locals.*

Mama was cutting Hannah's hair in the lodge's kitchen. Hannah's braid had grown far down her back, and Hannah decided she wanted her hair shorter and restyled for the rodeo. Besides, she was tired of the braid.

"What difference does it make?" Walt asked. "It's just a party—it wouldn't kill you to have her there."

"Yeah, my *birthday* party. Mama, I shouldn't have called her a jerk, but she...she thinks she's so much better than me. She probably wouldn't even want to come. I doubt we have anything in common. I mean she wears black nail polish and has tattoos."

"Hold still," Mama said.

"Tattoos?" Walt asked. He hadn't been there when Hannah had told Mama all about the fight. "Are you serious?"

"Walt, I'm trying to talk to Mama. Would you be quiet?"

"All right, but I bet they weren't really tattoos. Nobody's gonna give a thirteen-year-old a tattoo. They were probably those rub-on transfer ones you buy at the store." Walt poured himself another bowl of cereal—his evening snack.

"Well, they looked real," Hannah said, "and she acted like they were." What if they were fake and she had fallen for it? Serena would really think she didn't know anything.

"I don't think Serena's tattoos are the issue here," Mama said. She ran her fingers down the length of the sides of Hannah's hair. "What do you think, Hannah?"

"Feels even to me."

Mama smiled. "I mean, what do you think is the issue?"

"I already told you. We don't have anything in common."

"How do you know you don't?" Mama asked, trimming a little more. "You don't even know her yet."

Hannah sighed.

"Even if she doesn't become a good friend, do you really want to leave off as enemies?"

"So you're saying I have to invite her?"

"No. I'm saying, before you make your decision, think about this situation from Serena's point of view. But think fast. The party's Wednesday, you know."

Mama set down her scissors and picked up the hair dryer. "How about I style it?"

Hannah nodded. Mama blew and brushed. Finally, she smiled and passed Hannah the hand mirror for a look at her new hairdo.

"Not bad, twerp." Walt eyed Hannah's wavy, just-off-the-shoulders, thick strawberry blonde hair.

"Thanks!" Hannah's emerald eyes gleamed as Walt left the room. Some days even big brothers are okay. Hannah ran her thumb over her stubby fingernails. "Mama, Aunt Theresa says when you call someone a name it's a sign of pride. But I didn't feel proud."

"How did you feel?"

"I don't know. Stupid, I guess."

"How do you think Serena felt when she realized you had seen her singing and waving her feet in the air?"

"Probably stupid." Hannah laughed at the memory. "Really stupid."

"And do you think Serena means to be rude about Laketon? Have you told her that being called a local bothers you?"

"No."

"Maybe it's like how you and Papa say living in New York City would be like living in a box. You don't mean to be rude. It's just that it's so different from what you're used to."

"I guess," Hannah said. "But it sure seems like she thinks she's better."

"Maybe she does. But you don't always know why people say the things they do or act the way they do. You know, I had a big sister once."

"Had?"

"Oh, most people now see me and Theresa as about the same age. But I was your age then."

"So Aunt Theresa must've been about seven-teen," Hannah said, thinking.

"She could get very jealous if I got too fresh with a certain young man who drove an old convertible. He used to call me the cute kid sister."

"Uncle Joe?" Hannah giggled, lightly touching the ends of her newly trimmed hair with her finger-tips.

"One day he called me a pesty squirt. I think he wanted to let your aunt know he wasn't more fond of me than he was of her. It backfired."

"I'll bet!" Hannah raised an eyebrow. "Let me guess—you were both mad as hornets at him!"

"She was madder than I was! But my point about this is that Uncle Joe didn't really think I was a pest. He had a different reason for saying so."

"Funny," Hannah laughed. "Uncle Joe and Aunt Theresa didn't tell me that when we were talking about this stuff at dinner."

* * * * * * *

Hannah walked up the Shozenskis' front walk to the front door the next morning, her freshly cut hair windblown from the boat ride. After her conversa-tion with Mama, she had decided what she would do: She would apologize to Serena and invite her to her birthday party. What else could she do? With a shaky finger she pushed the doorbell. What if Serena was still mad? What if she thought she was dumb for thinking she'd want to come to her party?

The door swung open. It was Serena's older brother.

"Uh...uh is Serena home?" Hannah stammered.

"Yeah." He pointed over his shoulder at a wall.

Hannah assumed he meant that Serena was

over there and she should come in. She stepped inside and followed him around the corner.

"Someone's here," the boy said, stepping out of Hannah's way.

Hannah saw Serena sitting on the living room floor surrounded by pictures, colored paper, and markers.

Serena looked at her in surprise. "I figured it was someone for Steve."

Hannah stood in the doorway. "It's me. I...uh...I wanted to apologize for not using your front door yesterday and for getting mad at you."

"Really?" Serena fiddled with the rings on her right hand, her blonde hair falling forward to frame her face. Hannah bit her lip. Was Serena going to stay mad?

"You could sit down," Serena said. "I'm, um, working on a scrapbook of our summer vacations. My mom thought it would be a good project for me to do while we're here."

*While you're bored, you mean,* Hannah filled in. But she caught herself and didn't say it. Instead, she sat across from Serena on the floor, careful not to touch any of the pictures, careful not to look at them, either. She didn't want to be accused again of being a snoop. She crossed her legs like Serena had hers. They were both wearing old, faded jeans today.

"Serena, I—"

"Listen," Serena interrupted, "I'm sorry, too. I guess I'm not used to having people apologize to me. That's really cool." She smiled, not the big bright smile Hannah saw the day she met her, but a shy smile. "I guess I yelled at you first."

Hannah shrugged. "That's all right." Serena's brown eyes were so intense. *This wasn't supposed to be a big deal,* Hannah thought. *I just want to get this over with.* "Would you come—"

Just then the doorbell rang. "Just a minute," Serena said. She went to the door and came back with Caylin.

"Hi," Caylin said. "Oh, cool. You have your pictures out. I saw you come over here, Hannah, so I came over. Hannah! Is that really you? You have majorly changed. You look so...so grown up!"

"Her hair looks really good," Serena agreed.

"Have you found out yet when you're going home?" Caylin asked.

"Our new school is finally ready, so we're heading back to New Jersey in a couple days."

"Good," said Hannah.

Serena shot Hannah a dirty look.

"I...I mean it's great you're going to stay two more days. Can you come to my birthday party tomorrow night? That's what I came over to ask you."

"Oh?" Serena grinned the big, bright smile Hannah recognized. "I'd *love* to. But I have to ask my mom. And guys, I don't mean to be rude, but—" she looked at her watch—"my mom is taking me shopping in Skowhegan in ten minutes. I'm going to have to catch up with you later."

"No problem," Hannah said. "Just let me know. The party's at seven at my aunt and uncle's."

"Y' know, Han," Caylin said as they walked home, "I was beginning to think Serena did pretty much what she wanted to, but she had to ask her mom."

"Yeah." Hannah thought for a moment. "I guess her family has rules, too. I asked my mom and dad if they would let me dye my hair."

"You want to dye your hair?" Caylin shrieked.

"No," Hannah laughed, "but I was curious if they'd let me."

"What did they say?"

"They said no they wouldn't, but not to act as though Serena's family should have the same rule. And, of course, Papa said my hair is *bea-u-ti-ful* the way it is." Hannah giggled happily, remembering.

"You want to come over to my house?" Caylin asked.

"Can't," Hannah said. "I have to train with Ebony. I can't believe how close the rodeo's getting."

"So what are we going to do at your party?" Caylin teased. "Watch rodeo videos?"

Hannah laughed. "If I know Aunt Theresa, we're going to eat lots of good food."

"Hey, it is my birthday," Hannah said, laughing and tossing her hair when Serena suggested after the party that they all could swim from her float if it weren't so late in the season.

"I should say it's too late," huffed Aunt Theresa. "You'll catch a horrid cold. And look what time it is!"

Hannah shot a glance at her aunt's clock in the living room striking half past ten. The party guests had gone home, except Serena and Caylin. Mama was helping Aunt Theresa wash dishes, while Hannah, Walt, and the two girls listened to a CD that Hannah had received as a gift.

"No ice on the lake yet, Auntie," Hannah laughed, though she knew Moosehead Lake was cold after Labor Day.

Aunt Theresa was not ready for crazy ideas, so she did not answer.

"You're too chicken to try it," Walt teased.

"Wanna bet! Remember us diving down to the wreck of the *President Lincoln* in November?"

"That's different. We had wet suits on."

"You're the chicken, Walt!"

"Hey, I'm not afraid o' cold water. But me'n Mama and Papa are heading back for the island right away."

"We have lights, and our float's still in the lake." Serena sounded as though she actually meant it.

"There was frost on the grass this morning," Caylin protested.

"Oh c'mon. Why don't you go home and get your suit?" Serena grinned. "Like my dad always says, you only live once."

"Well," Hannah said, "I've got a swimsuit upstairs. Wanna do it, Caylin?"

Mama walked into the living room just then. "Harry, don't you think we should be heading back for Beaver Island?" To Hannah she said, "If you're going for a dip, be sure to take a sweatshirt. You'll be cold as a codfish when you climb out." To Hannah's surprise, Mama did not suggest that the girls not go swimming.

Papa grinned, shaking his head.

Hannah was so startled she did not answer Mama.

"I'm gonna go get my suit on," Serena shrieked. She was really warming up to the idea. "When you see our back lights come on, head over. This will be totally fun!"

"This will be totally cold," Caylin said.

"Swimming in the rain, oh I'm swimming in the rain," Serena sang ten minutes later.

"You're crazy," Hannah laughed.

The girls raced out the long ramp to the

Shozenskis' float. It had started to drizzle. Serena, Hannah noticed, no longer had any tattoos.

"Got your suit on under your clothes?" Hannah eyed Caylin's jeans and sweatshirt.

"Naw. I'm just gonna watch." Caylin hugged herself to keep warm.

Hannah shrugged. "Suit yourself, but I wish you would."

"KER-SPLASH!" Serena jumped from the dock with a whoop. She bobbed up seconds later and scrambled up the ladder.

"How's the water?" asked Hannah.

"C-c-cold," Serena admitted. She flipped the wet fingers of both hands into their faces.

"Yikes!" The freezing water stung Hannah's bare shoulders.

"Let's throw her in! Caylin, give me a hand!" Serena grabbed for Hannah, and Caylin pretended to try to help.

"You'll have to catch me!" Hannah raced onto the springboard and dove off. The lake water of early fall, like tiny ice picks, stabbed every pore of Hannah's body. By the time she surfaced, though, her pores had closed, and a sensation of warmth ran up her spine.

Hannah climbed the ladder to the dock. She shivered as the cold night air now attacked her wet skin.

"You cracked the ice on the lake," Caylin joked. "Now you're turning blue as a mackerel."

"Blue, schmoo! How can you tell? It's too dark out here. You're just chicken."

"Am not. You're crazy. Don't you think you better put your sweatshirt on like your mother said?"

Hannah strolled toward her sweatshirt, which she'd left hanging on a life preserver. Two could tease. Passing Caylin, she suddenly tackled the older but smaller girl around the middle. Caylin struggled and screeched, but Hannah leaped off the dock.

A very wet, very cold, very angry Caylin beat Hannah to the ladder and scrambled out. "I'll *never* come to one of your crummy parties again!" she yelled.

"Hey, Caylin, I'm sorry, okay? Just put my new sweatshirt on and wear it home. No big deal."

"This one?" Caylin grabbed the new fleece-lined green shirt with a bull moose on the front. It was a birthday present. She flung the sweatshirt into the black water, then raced for home. "If I get sick again, it's your fault," she called back.

Hannah leaped in to save her shirt. *If she gets sick again? Oh, no! I forgot she's had a sore throat.*

"What was wrong with Caylin?" Serena asked as Hannah climbed out. "Usually she's a lot of fun."

"Usually," Hannah said. Shivering, she wrung out the sweatshirt. Caylin should have told them why she wasn't going swimming, Hannah reasoned. Was she really supposed to remember every little sniffle Caylin had?

Then she had an awful thought. What if Caylin missed the pageant because of her?

Over and over again in Hannah's head echoed Caylin's threat, *I'm never coming to one of your crummy parties again!*

# Chapter Twelve

# The Star of the Pageant

"Caylin home, Mrs. Coulson?"

Hannah was not at all surprised when Caylin did not come over to Aunt Theresa's house to visit the afternoon following the birthday party. After her studies, Hannah had taken Ebony for a tough workout at the club. Ebony was striding long and tight around the barrels, and he hadn't touched a single one. 16.2 seconds! It should have been a great day, but Hannah kept remembering her fight with Caylin. They had never had a big fight before, and Hannah wanted it to end. She had come to apologize.

"Neat sweatshirt! I'll bet you got it for your birthday," Mrs. Coulson said. She eyed Hannah's shirt with the moose. Aunt Theresa's dryer had left the shirt as fluffy as new after being soaked in the lake.

Hannah stood on one foot, then the other. Somehow she did not wish to remind Mrs. Coulson that she hadn't answered her question. Mrs. Coulson must know that she pulled Caylin into the lake.

"Caylin's gone to Skowhegan with her father." Mrs. Coulson smiled. "I'm sorry she missed you. I'll be sure to let her know you stopped by."

"She's okay, I hope. I mean, she doesn't have a cold or anything?"

"Oh, no, at least we don't think so. She's had a scratchy throat for several weeks already. It's no better, so she's seeing a throat specialist. Her father has another job interview."

"I'm sorry. Well...I'll be praying for them." Hannah tried hard to act upbeat.

Hannah felt miserable as she walked back to Aunt Theresa's house and slipped up the back stairs to her room. She sulked on her bed for a while, staring out the window at the Coulson house. *Guilt.* Why should she feel guilty? She had just been trying to have fun. She certainly was sorry. Sorry for throwing Caylin in. Sorry that Caylin's dad had lost his job in Laketon. Sorry that Caylin had to go to the doctor. But Hannah was also sorry that Caylin was not home when she went over to apologize.

Hannah stood before the dresser mirror and began angrily to brush the kinks out of her new, grownup hair. *If I still had that French braid I wouldn't need to do this a dozen times a day,* she thought. *Why did I ever ask Mama to cut it?*

*Why?* —it seemed to be the question of the day. Why couldn't she have just had a nice birthday?

Caylin should have told them why she didn't want to go swimming. *Does she expect everyone to remember she was sick?* Hannah had other things to think about besides her. *Besides,* Hannah thought, *Mrs. Coulson said herself that Caylin's been sick already for several weeks. What I did has nothing to do with anything. But what if Caylin's serious? What if she really will blame me if she misses the pageant? But she won't miss the pageant,* Hannah told herself. *She totally overreacted to the whole thing. Besides, she owes me an apology. She ruined my birthday—an awful fight after a perfect day!*

Hannah picked up a Western magazine from the table beside her bed. She decided friends had to be understanding. When Caylin came home, she'd go over and talk to her. After all, they were best buds.

It was after seven o'clock when Hannah finally saw Caylin and her dad come home. She waited a while, then went over.

"Caylin's in her room," Mrs. Coulson said, frowning. She nodded toward the hall. "Go on in."

"Thanks," Hannah said.

"Caylin, Hannah's here." Caylin's mom sounded worried.

Caylin opened her door. She looked cozy in her sweatsuit and slippers. "Hi, come in."

"Hi." Hannah stepped inside Caylin's familiar, tidy room. "I've been so worried. How's your throat?"

"The doctor's loading me up with antibiotics—I have tonsillitis."

"Will...will you be able to sing?"

"I think so. But I gotta keep drinking lots of liquids and spraying my throat." Caylin pointed to a bottle of medicine with a spray pump on her dresser. "I guess I'd *better*, with what I spent for my clothes. I just hope Aunt Theresa doesn't get stage fright. I'm so excited, Hannah."

"Oh, Caylin!" Hannah squeezed her and kissed her cheek. "I'll be right in the front row cheering."

Caylin grinned. "Not to worry," she said, seeing Hannah frown. "Tonsillitis isn't catching, like a cold. But I've gotta have my tonsils out in the hospital in Skowhegan sometime soon."

"Once you win the Miss Lakeland contest, you're supposed to be in the big pageant at the fair. You've *gotta* stay healthy!"

"Oh, I won't win Miss Lakeland." Caylin shrugged. "Everyone else has lived here forever. People in Laketon probably don't even know who I am."

"Tell me about it! When you live on an island in the lake like me, people think you don't belong around here. But Caylin, you *will* win! That night you sang at the lodge—you'd win *any* contest!"

"Thanks."

Hannah plunked down on Caylin's bed. "I'm sorry about last night."

Caylin shrugged. "It's okay."

"I am so nervous," Hannah said. "The rodeo's only eight days away. You gotta meet us there."

"Definitely. My mom and dad said we'd go."

"And you gotta come watch me and Ebony tomorrow. I think we'll set our record time."

"I should be resting and practicing tomorrow."

"Please, come for a little while?"

"Hannah, if you want me to perform in the pageant Saturday, I can't."

"Oh." Hannah thought Caylin should be able to spare at least an hour.

Hannah sat atop Ebony. She remembered thinking how Kennie MacKenzie looked like she was a part of her horse, like she lived in the saddle. Hannah felt that way about Ebony now. She couldn't count how many hours she had spent practicing.

"Hey daydreamer," Uncle Joe called. "Let's see what you and Ebony can do today."

"I'm scared," Hannah called back. "What if he

doesn't do as good as yesterday? Yesterday was perfect."

"You can't win a race on yesterday. Let's get going. If you had held onto Ebony's best time last week, you wouldn't know how good he'd get this week, *non?*"

"You're right, Uncle Joe." Hannah trotted Ebony to the beginning mark. She leaned forward and stroked his neck. "Come on, Ebony." She sighted their course around the barrels. She looked Uncle Joe's way to let him know she was ready.

Uncle Joe held out the stopwatch. "Go!" he shouted.

And they shot away. Hannah could hear Uncle Joe cheering her on and shouting directions. "Give him his head—now, now! That's it!"

"Not a single barrel touched," Uncle Joe shouted as they finished. He grinned. "Not too close, not too wide. The corners looked good. Just a tad slower than yesterday's best."

Hannah swung off of Ebony and ran over to Uncle Joe. "I'm really doing it!"

He gave her a high five. "Now just do zat at ze rodeo next Friday, okay?"

"I will," Hannah said. "Just wait."

Uncle Joe reached inside his jacket. "I have something for you." His eyes twinkled.

"What is it?" Hannah loved surprises.

Uncle Joe pulled out a brown leather quirt, one of the small riding whips barrel racers use. "Just like Kennie MacKenzie has."

"Cool."

Uncle Joe put the soft leather handle in Hannah's hand. "You know how to use it, right?"

"Yeah—hey, look, Serena's coming." Hannah waved. "I wonder if she wants to watch me practice."

Serena jogged over to them, a camera in her

hand. "Hi," she said breathlessly. "My mom and dad decided to leave now instead of in the morning. I wanted to say goodbye."

"I'm glad you found me." Hannah eyed her white school T-shirt with all the signatures. "I wish you could stay for the rodeo."

"Me too, but I'm also excited to get home. Hey, I wanted to take a picture of you and Ebony—for our scrapbook."

"Not me?" Uncle Joe teased.

"No, not you," Serena laughed. "Come on, Hannah, let's go over by those trees."

Hannah walked beside Serena, holding Ebony's reins with one hand, fingering her new riding quirt with the other. "You coming back next summer?"

"I think so."

"Good," Hannah said. She then realized she really meant it.

Hannah wore her new Stetson hat, Western shirt, and hand-tooled riding boots to the Miss Lakeland contest at Laketon High Saturday evening. *Maybe I shouldn't have worn this outfit,* Hannah worried, looking around. The crowd filled even the bleachers. *People might notice me, and this is supposed to be Caylin's show tonight, not mine,* she mused. She had decided to sit with her parents instead of the girls she knew from church and Laketon Christian Academy. *Funny how staying away from home makes me want to be with my parents.*

Hannah waited anxiously through the performances. The contestants had drawn straws, and she knew Caylin didn't perform until last. As she watched the girls play flutes and violins, dance ballet, and sing, Hannah began to see that this wasn't just a beauty contest. These girls were talented—except for one who had sung completely off-key. They had to be brave to perform in front of the whole town.

By the time Aunt Theresa took her place at the old upright piano for Caylin's turn, Hannah almost wished she had entered the pageant, too. It was like a dare: Could she be that brave? Besides, it looked like fun, beyond the fear.

Aunt Theresa started playing. The piano was in tune, but it was tinny. *This is awful,* Hannah fretted.

Then Auntie began to play "Home on the Range," a number Hannah knew she and Caylin had practiced.

But Caylin did not come onstage.

Aunt Theresa played another stanza, adding trills and runs.

Still no Caylin.

Hannah clung to her seat, fighting an urge to run backstage. Shuffling feet made the auditorium noisy.

Aunt Theresa frowned, looking into the wings. Hannah then saw Caylin's mom, who held up a sign. *Uh-oh!* Hannah realized that her nervous aunt had played the wrong song!

Aunt Theresa nodded at Mrs. Coulson, then finished the stanza she was playing. As Aunt Theresa switched to "Clementine," an old gold-rush song, Caylin swept prettily onto the stage. Her red hair shone like burnished bronze beneath her straw topper. Red lipstick set off her alabaster skin—made all the whiter, Hannah feared—because she had been sick. Caylin was petite, but when she opened her mouth, the words came out in a full-throated contralto—a BIG voice, Hannah decided at once.

The crowd was enraptured. When Caylin got to the line, "You are lost and gone forever, dreadful sorry, Clementine," Caylin sobbed real tears that she dried with a lace handkerchief.

The crowd leaped to their feet, clapping the minute the last note came from Caylin's throat. They stomped. They cheered. A couple of guys in the bleachers hooted and whistled.

"Yea!" "Great!" "Encore!" came from several corners of the gymnasium.

"Amen!" shouted Uncle Joe from the front row.

As soon as the crowd settled down, the judges announced: "Miss Lakeland of the Moosehead Lake Region—Miss Caylin Coulson!" Over the cheering, Hannah could barely hear the next announcement: "The new Miss Lakeland will represent Laketon and Piscataquis County at the Texas Mesquite Miss of Maine contest next week in Skowhegan!"

Hannah climbed to the platform to hug Caylin. Both girls grinned and linked arms as cameras flashed and camcorder lights flooded the stage.

Hannah imagined for just a moment that this was the crowd at the rodeo, and they were all clapping for her.

# Chapter Thirteen

# Hamstring Harvey

"I can't believe it," Hannah said. "We're actually leaving for the fair."

Walt grinned. "I know. Tomorrow night, under the arena lights, we're going to be in the rodeo. Crowds of people, wild bulls, rodeo announcers..."

"Stop it," Hannah laughed. "You're making me nervous."

Uncle Joe's horse trailer, with a pile of equipment next to it, was hitched to his pickup. Saddle, hay, sleeping bags, backpacks.

"Help me get the ramp down, Walt. She is heavy," Uncle Joe said. He pulled the big steel pin that held the trailer's loading ramp.

"I'll go lead Ebony out!" Hannah cried.

"Are you kids still sure you don't want to stay with my friends in Skowhegan? Uncle Joe plans to stay with a friend, you know." Mama cast a worried glance at Hannah as Uncle Joe loaded Ebony. She handed Walt the sleeping bags to stash behind the truck seat.

"Oh, Mama! Lots of kids with 4-H Club agricultural projects sleep right in the barn with their

115

steers and sheep," Hannah protested. "Besides, I've got my big brother to protect me." She punched Walt's shoulder.

"I suppose. But it's a different world out there than when I grew up in Skowhegan. Papa and I will come first thing tomorrow morning, so we could take you to the stables in plenty of time."

"There's nothing to worry about, Mama," Hannah laughed.

"I think that's fifteen fried elephant ears you've swallowed—one for every year of your life!" Hannah teased Walt that evening.

"Not quite. But I've had three hot dogs, all with raw onions."

"You'll barf, most likely."

"So be it," Walt laughed. "They sure tasted good going down."

"Don't ask me to sit next to you on the ferris wheel, bear breath!" As Walt stepped up to the ticket booth, Hannah craned her neck for a better look at the huge, lighted wheel turning slowly in the starry night sky.

"Then you won't want me anywhere near you tonight in the stables, either," Walt teased. "I'm here to protect my baby sis, remember?"

"I guess in the horse stables it won't make much difference. There are other smells there that a lady doesn't talk about."

After riding the ferris wheel, Hannah and Walt headed back toward the barns.

"How's Ebony after his trailer ride?" Walt asked.

"He'll be okay once he's had a night's rest," Hannah said confidently. "And so will I," she added, remembering the restful nights she'd had sleeping in Papa's haymow in the barn on Beaver Island. "We get two practices tomorrow."

"Uncle Joe, you don't have to do *that,*" Hannah cried as she and Walt entered the stables. "Tendin' Ebony's *my* job."

"Your job is to win that barrel ridin' contest. I'm ze stable boy whenever I'm here," he chuckled, winking at Walt.

"Well, all right," Hannah laughed. "Just remember who's supposed to ride him.... HEY!" She grabbed a garden hose hanging by a water bucket and squirted a cigarette butt smoldering in the straw between the stalls.

"Watch it!" Walt jumped aside, his jeans dripping and wet.

"Some people can't read!" Hannah pointed toward a sign that said "No Smoking" in English and *"Defense de Fumer"* in French.

"I thought I smelled smoke," said Uncle Joe. "You were quick, *non?*"

Walt peeled his cold jeans away from his skin, realizing now why Hannah had used the hose.

A skinny man in ratty jeans and a tattered shirt stood at the far end of the aisle. He lit a cigarette, squinted at Hannah, then strolled outside, walking toward the rodeo arena.

"He gives me the creeps." Hannah shuddered. "I'll bet he was the one who dropped that butt."

"He doesn't belong in the stables, or he wouldn't be smoking," Uncle Joe said. "Don't worry about him, though. The police clear the fairgrounds of people who don't have special passes like us soon as the midway closes each evening. Now I have to get going. I promised my friend I'd be there about now."

"Walt," Hannah whispered. They were stretched out in their sleeping bags on top of hay bales piled in the walkway between the horse stalls.

"What is it this time? I just got to sleep." Too many fried elephant ear pastries and grilled hot dogs with onions, and anxiety about the rodeo the next night, were giving Walt a hard night.

"That man." Hannah pointed toward a shadowy figure, a man in a billed cap, several stalls away.

"So? He's just another horse farmer. Probably going out to the bathroom. Go back to sleep."

"I can't." And Hannah couldn't. Tomorrow morning she would practice with Ebony. Tomorrow night, under lights, she'd compete in the big Texas Mesquite Rodeo. Hannah had watched that afternoon as riders in trucks with plates from Texas and several other Western states unloaded dozens of horses over by the racehorse paddock. Hannah hadn't seen any Wyoming plates, but she hadn't really believed she'd get to compete against Kennie MacKenzie anyway. But if she got to Texas, she dreamed, maybe she would.

Only folks from Maine farms used the agricultural stables where she and Walt were trying to sleep next to Ebony's stall. Hannah had toured the stables, making friends with the farm kids until she could find her way around in the dark. Besides a few riding horses brought in by Maine country folks who hoped to compete in the rodeo against seasoned Texas cowboys and cowgirls, there were dozens of huge draft horses to compete all day in the pulling contests. Hannah had also seen pairs of oxen and prize dairy cows by the hundred, besides carefully groomed sheep, and washed, perfumed pigs, the pride of 4-H Club kids from all over Maine out to win blue ribbons.

Hannah smelled cigarette smoke. She squirmed around in her sleeping bag for a better look. Real farmers did not smoke in barns, she knew. But it could be someone standing outside.

A man leaned against the post near the entrance, outlined in the big floodlight just outside. He was tall and skinny and wore a coat with the collar turned up, a billed cap, and cowboy boots. *Looks like the same guy Walt said was heading for the bathroom.* Hannah poked a button on her watch, and the dial lit up. A quarter past two. *I suppose he's nervous and can't sleep either. Probably like me, competing tomorrow night.* A red glow then lit the man's face. *At least he's smoking outside,* thought Hannah.

Hannah buried her head in her pillow, trying to stop all her thoughts about the rodeo. Finally, she dozed off.

"SNAP!" Hannah was jerked awake by a sharp clink of metal against metal in the quiet night. She raised her head.

The skinny man in cowboy boots stood by a horse pen. Hannah couldn't see exactly what he was doing, but the man was holding a large, two-handled tool that looked in the dark like Papa's pruning shears.

Hannah shook Walt's shoulders. "Sshhh! Look! Don't say anything."

Walt raised his head.

Then the man flicked on a cigarette lighter. Hannah and Walt watched as the fellow quietly laid his two-handled tool in the straw, then picked a broken padlock from the lock on the gate of the pen.

"Why's he doin' that when he can just climb over?" Hannah whispered.

"He needs a way to scram real quick." Walt was thinking fast.

The skinny guy held his lighter up for a better look. He quietly opened the gate.

Walt unzipped his sleeping bag.

Hannah unzipped hers.

The zippers seemed loud in the quiet barn.

The man flicked his lighter on again.

Hannah watched in horror, knowing he must be planning to hurt the two beautiful, big Belgian horses inside the stall. But why?

Hunkered down in the straw, the fellow pulled a long knife from the top of a boot. He half crouched, then turned to enter the stall.

The next thing Hannah knew, Walt was out of his bag.

"Walt, he's got a knife!" Hannah screamed.

The man popped out of the pen.

Walt tackled the fellow by the legs.

Hannah grabbed a pitchfork from a bale of hay.

The man fell, then rolled. He and Walt were on their knees, facing each other. The fellow still had his knife, but Walt held his wrist.

Hannah raised the fork. Her joints seemed filled with glue. Everything went into slow motion as she raised the pitchfork higher, higher.

The man yanked his knife hand free from Walt's grip.

*Now or...!* Hannah swung. Hard! The pitchfork handle struck the man's head.

"I hope I didn't hurt him," Hannah gasped. She was shaking. It felt terrible to hit someone. The fellow lay silent at her feet on his side, not moving.

"You got him good, miss," growled a stout man

in bib overalls, as the lights came on. Cursing, the man in overalls rolled the skinny man over. The skinny man groaned and opened his eyes. "It's him, all right, sheriff—Hamstring Harvey. We staked out the wrong stable. If it hadn't been fer these here kids, he'd 'a ruined my hosses! Guess I should've stayed and guarded them, but I had no idea they'd be targeted."

"Why it's..."

"The same guy who dropped that cigarette this afternoon." Walt finished Hannah's sentence.

A tall man with a silver badge pinned to his suspenders yanked Harvey to his feet and snapped handcuffs on his wrists. Harvey started to struggle.

More lights came on, as sleepers woke up. Horses nickered and stamped around.

"You won't be needing this," the sheriff growled as he fished a roll of fifty-dollar bills from Harvey's hip pocket. "You got paid in advance. It'll be interesting to see whose prints are on this money!"

The big man who owned the horses glared at Harvey. "You bet it will be interesting."

"Miss Parmenter," the sheriff said, as soon as Hannah and Walt gave him their names, "you'll have to excuse me. I'll need to talk with you about this tomorrow."

The sheriff left with Hamstring Harvey, and the big man sat on a bale of hay staring angrily at his pen of workhorses.

Hannah sat down on her sleeping bag. "What's 'hamstring' mean, Walt?"

"To cut a horse's tendons and make it lame." Walt was so mad he shook. Together they eyed the grand pair of Belgian pulling horses the skinny man had been messing with.

"But why would...?" Then she understood. "You

mean, that Harvey guy was being *paid* to cripple somebody's horses!"

"If you hadn't yelled, I could have jumped him from the pen wall before he knew I was on him," Walt complained.

"He had a knife, Walt! I saved your life, you big dumb ox! You were supposed to protect *me*—remember?"

"Yeah, I know. You sure swing a wild pitchfork." Walt eyed the fork next to Hannah's sleeping bag. "I doubt we can, but we better try to sleep if we're going to compete tomorrow."

"Yeah, right. I wish Papa were here. This thing gave me the creeps." Hannah climbed into her sleeping bag, zipped it up, and pulled it close around her. She was mad and scared and excited for tomorrow all at the same time.

At least she didn't have to worry about Ebony. He was safe in his stall right beside her. She would just have to put it out of her mind. She had a race to win, and nothing was going to get in her way. Nothing.

# Chapter Fourteen

# Rodeo Danger

"Run the part with Kennie MacKenzie again, Walt."

Uncle Joe had rented a twenty-inch TV and VCR and set them up in the barn next to Ebony's stall. "It'll calm you two to see your events done right one last time," he had said. Now, bored with tending their sheep and pigs, several kids slightly younger than Hannah had come to watch.

Walt ejected one tape and put in another. "One more time through Kennie. After that I want to watch steer wrestling."

"No fair, Walt. I've watched it only a couple of times."

"And a bunch of other barrel racers before that."

"Walt's in the rodeo, too, *non?*" Uncle Joe said.

Hannah nodded, and Uncle Joe meandered down the barn aisle to admire the different animals. Hannah leaned forward on her hay bale seat, ready to watch closely.

Walt pressed the fast-forward button to speed Uncle Joe's tape past the ads.

"Why'd ya do that? I wanted t'see the ad with that cute baby," complained a girl from the sheep pens.

"It's *our* show," Hannah said. "We'll watch it however we please!"

"I hear your sheep bleating for you," Walt added. "Why don't you go tend 'em?"

"What's it to ya?" bristled a boy.

"I mean it! Keep still or scram!"

"Pigs!" The girl hurried off.

"Yeah!" agreed the boy. "You're both selfish!"

"Your new friends left quick, *non?*" said Uncle Joe, walking up when he saw them leave in a hurry.

"Buncha pests!" Walt growled.

"They *were* giving us a hard time," Hannah agreed. "We're not here to babysit. Maybe I shouldn't have been mean to them, Uncle Joe, but I'm scared."

"You didn't do nothin' wrong, honey," Uncle Joe soothed. "It sounds like you two could have told them more kindly to leave, but you've got a right to watch that video without bein' pestered most to death."

"Maybe I was too rough," Walt said, "but their whining got on my nerves."

"And we hardly got any sleep last night." Hannah glanced toward an empty pen with a small sign that said, "Lew Robinson—Champion Pulling Belgians." Hannah and Walt had told Uncle Joe about Hamstring Harvey as soon as he got to the fairgrounds that morning.

Uncle Joe nodded. "You both have a lot on your minds. I'll ask the sheriff's office to leave you alone until after the rodeo."

"Good," Hannah said. "I tried to watch your video and concentrate on the moves. But those noisy kids from all over the stables just pounced on us like...like crows after roadkill. I've got knots in my stomach!" Hannah wiped a stray tear on her sleeve.

"*Oui.* Mebbe your circuits are overloaded from so much going on."

"I can take the excitement," Hannah said, "but I just *have* to win this race."

"There's an old song," Uncle Joe said, "'Hear ye—'"

"I know," Hannah interrupted. She sang the song she had heard her uncle singing many times as he worked:

"Hear ye the Master's call,
'Give me thy best!'
For, be it great or small,
That is His test.
Do then the best you can,
Not for reward,
Not for the praise of man,
But for the Lord."

"That's the spirit!" Uncle Joe laughed. "When we're doing it for Jesus we can get our minds off ourselves, *non?*"

"Right, Uncle Joe," Hannah said. "But my best better be good enough. I just have to win this race."

"Our singing cowgirl needs a guitar and a stage!" Just then Papa strode up with Mama and Aunt Theresa.

"What she needs right now is a change of clothes and a hot bath!" put in Mama. "Papa and I have rented a room at the Elmwood Motel across the street, since it'll be too late to drive home after the rodeo. Sam and Judy Sampson are tending Beaver Lodge for us tonight. Hannah, your clean clothes are in the motel room. The best thing you can do now is to soak in a tub of hot water until you loosen up."

"But I need to take care of Ebony, and we'll have to practice," Hannah protested.

"*After* you've had a hot bath and a decent breakfast," Mama insisted.

"Your mother's right—there's plenty of time." Papa grinned and nodded toward the motel.

"All right," Hannah said. "I'll go." She hardly thought she had plenty of time, but she knew Mama and Papa were right. A good breakfast would give her the energy she needed to ride a winning race.

*Are we still in Maine?* Hannah pondered, looking around the fairgrounds' outdoor horse arena under the nighttime floodlights. Country and Western music played over the loudspeaker. Earlier, when she had ridden Ebony past here on her way to practice, this arena was crowded with farmers in billed caps and jeans or bibbed overalls. The farmers had been watching heavy horse- and ox-pulling contests.

"Look at all the Stetson hats and cowboy boots, Mama," Hannah cried.

"When there's a rodeo, everybody tries to dress Western," Mama chuckled. "I'm sure Joe's been looking forward to it!"

"Yes, ma'am." Uncle Joe tipped the brim of his cowboy hat at Mama. He was wearing his usual flannel shirt, but he had bought a hat for the occasion.

"We should have got Harry a cowboy hat, too," Aunt Theresa chuckled.

Papa smiled. "Thanks, but I'm more comfortable

without one, I think. C'mon. Let's all get ringside seats."

Papa led Mama, Hannah, Aunt Theresa, and Uncle Joe down an aisle to a block of empty seats below the grandstand bleachers.

Aunt Theresa leaned forward around Hannah. "Remember how we used to bug Mom and Dad to bring us to the fair at night, Sandy? It seemed more special at night than during the day."

"It still does," Mama said. Distracted, she looked toward the chutes. "I hope Walt found the contestants' area okay."

"I'm sure he did," Uncle Joe assured her. "There will be rodeo folks back there letting them know what to do."

"I'm glad steer wrestling's first, not barrel racing," Hannah said. Barrel racing was in the middle. Hannah was just sitting out here until after Walt's race. Then she would have to hurry back to the holding areas with Ebony to line up.

Her breakfast of scrambled eggs and pancakes and a fair hamburger lunch had long since worn off. She'd been too nervous to eat dinner, even though Mama had unsuccessfully insisted. Now she didn't know whether the smell of the vendors' popcorn, hamburgers, and onion-covered hot dogs made her feel hungry or sick to her stomach.

Hannah thought it was funny how, to the people watching, the rodeo was just entertainment. The folks grabbed snacks like she would before a ball game. *Don't they know I'll be racing in a little while?* The silly question flitted through her head. Just on the other side of the livestock barns, as if nothing else were happening, people were still going on rides: the hammer, the pirate ship, the roller coaster, the ring of fire. Hannah could see the bright lights twinkling, flashing hot pink, orange, white, green.

Hannah craned her neck to look around. "Where on earth are Caylin and her parents? They said they'd meet us here fifteen minutes ago."

"Waiting in line to buy tickets, no doubt," Papa said. "Good thing we got ours in advance."

Mama sighed. "Don't worry, honey. There are plenty of seats." She patted Hannah's new haircut.

Seats surrounded the arena except for the end on Hannah's left, where the holding areas and chutes were. But the seats were filling up fast. Hannah looked into the arena and imagined where the barrels would be. She had practiced the clover-leaf course so much she could probably place the barrels at the perfect distances and angles herself without measuring. Determined to be prepared even in the midst of all this distraction, Hannah lost herself in imagining the race.

Abruptly, the country and Western music stopped. "Welcome to the Mesquite Texas Rodeo, in Maine!" It was a man's voice on the loudspeaker, but Hannah couldn't see where he was. "Julia Bolduc of Bangor, Maine, will sing the national anthem. Would you all please stand?"

With a noisy shuffling of feet, everyone stood and faced the flag at the end of the arena. A woman wearing a red dress entered the ring and stood below the flag. As she sang, the crowd fell silent. When the singer reached the last line, a shiver went down Hannah's spine.

"Thank you, Mrs. Bolduc!" the announcer said over the crowd's applause. "Now, are you all ready for a wild time?"

People stomped their feet and shouted.

Hannah grinned at Mama. This was it!

"I knew you were ready! We'll have steer

wrestling, calf roping, barrel racing, bull riding, bronc riding—everything you could want in a rodeo! And now the first steer wrestler, Mark Benson of Terry, Montana!"

Three chutes opened, and two mounted horses with a steer between them charged out. One rider kept the steer in line as the other slid from his horse onto the steer's shoulders and wrestled him to the ground. The wrestler let the animal up and scrambled away quickly, out of the animal's path. A rodeo clown wearing a purple shirt, torn overalls cut into shorts, and red striped tights chased the steer through a gate back into the pens.

When Walt's name was announced, Hannah could barely stay in her seat. She exchanged glances with Mama as the chutes opened and the horses and steer shot out.

"Get 'im, Walt!" Hannah whooped and yelled. For a moment she forgot to worry about her barrel race or even wonder about Caylin.

Walt slid off his horse onto the steer's shoulders just like he was supposed to. Mama snapped pictures.

Walt hung onto the steer's horns, one arm across the steer's neck, his legs stretched out in front of him. But instead of Walt's wrestling him down, the steer was pulling Walt down the arena. Walt's right hand slipped, and Walt fell into the path of the angry animal. Walt jumped up, but as the steer tried to get away, he knocked Walt down again. Walt tried to roll clear, but as the steer ran past him, he stepped on Walt's leg.

The crowd gasped.

Walt lay in the dirt.

Two clowns ran the steer away and chased him into a chute.

Papa leaped the fence and raced toward Walt.

Two medical rescue workers ran into the arena from beneath the bleachers.

Hannah gripped Mama's hand.

Walt sat up. Pain shot across his face as he collapsed again.

Papa said something to Walt, holding his shoulders as the medics knelt over him. One cut away the jeans from his right leg. A third medical worker wheeled a stretcher beside them.

"Excuse me, excuse me," Mama said as she, Hannah, Aunt Theresa, and Uncle Joe pushed past the other people in their row to get to where a waiting ambulance had backed up next to the arena behind the pens. They hurried through the murmuring crowd, out of the grandstands, and around the far end of the arena. They couldn't see Walt or Papa. Mama gripped Hannah's hand so tightly it hurt.

*Protect him, Lord, and don't let him be afraid.* Prayers shot through Hannah's mind, and she knew Mama and Uncle Joe and Aunt Theresa were praying, too. She noticed funny things, like the dropped popcorn crunching into the dirt under her feet.

Now Hannah could see Papa standing beside Walt as the medics lifted Walt carefully onto the lowered stretcher.

"It appears that Walt Parmenter has broken his leg," the announcer said over the loudspeaker. "We are sorry, Walt. Rodeo is a dangerous sport. Walt will be taken care of, and then the rodeo will continue. Thank you all for your patience."

"A broken leg. That's awful, but thank God it's not worse," Mama said. She dropped Hannah's hand and fell into step with Papa, walking beside Walt as the medics carried the stretcher from the rodeo circle. Papa put his arm around Mama's shoulders.

Hannah cringed. Walt's leg was bent really weird.

"Oh, Walt," Mama said. "I'm so sorry."

"It hurts, Mama," Walt said through clenched teeth. "But they say it's just my leg." He gasped in pain. "At least I didn't get gored." He attempted a smile at Papa.

The medics paused before lifting Walt into the ambulance. "Anybody riding with him?"

"Harry, we've *got* to go with our boy."

Papa looked at Hannah, then back at Mama. "It's only a broken leg." Papa spoke calmly, though his eyes reflected pain and dismay. "Hannah needs one of us here at the event." Papa glanced worriedly at the ambulance.

"*Only* a broken leg?" Hannah asked.

"Uncle Joe and I will be here for your performance, dear," Aunt Theresa offered.

"Are you *sure* there are no internal injuries, Harry?"

"The medics checked, and I checked myself. Not a scratch except for his leg. That's the only place the steer stepped, and his horns didn't touch him."

Mama's tearful eyes searched Papa's face. "Harry, if you're *sure* Walt will be all right, will you go with him? I'll stay here with Hannah. She needs *one* of us. And we'll come right away afterward."

Papa half smiled. "I couldn't ask you *not* to go to the hospital, Sandy."

"You're going! I'm staying!" Mama answered fiercely. "Now get going! Take care of our boy!"

"We're praying for you," Mama said, as they lifted Walt into the ambulance.

Papa hugged Hannah and kissed her forehead, then climbed in after Walt.

"Skowhegan Hospital," the medic said, closing the ambulance doors.

"Skowhegan," Mama repeated.

The ambulance's lights flashed as it pulled out of the fairgrounds.

"Dear Lord, watch over Walt—and give me strength!" Hannah prayed aloud. She didn't know how she was ever going to concentrate on her race after this, and she felt bad for caring about her own race after Walt's accident, but this is what she had worked so hard for. And surely Walt would be okay.

Hannah stood just outside the arena, in shock at everything that had happened. Of course someone needed to go with Walt, but now Papa wouldn't get to see her race. Hannah felt like she was going to dissolve into tears. Inside, the rodeo announcer was already announcing the next steer-wrestling contestant.

"Let's pray," Uncle Joe said, putting his arm around her shoulder. "For Walt, for you, for all of us. Let's commit the rest of this day to the Lord."

# Chapter Fifteen

# Black Lightning

Hannah looked past the bright floodlights. Dusk had changed to night, and only a few faint stars peeped out. Ebony stepped around, fidgeting. "I know, I know." Hannah stroked his powerful neck. "You want to ride, feller."

Hannah's senses were full of the constant announcing, the clang of starting gates, the yells of the crowd. A rodeo official, Bob, led riders from the holding area to the starting gate. One by one, the riders returned.

"Another outstanding ride by young Jesse Hawkins!" crackled the loudspeaker. "The new time to beat is 16.0!"

"Great job!" Bob said as Jesse rode back.

"Thanks." Jesse grinned and flipped her braid over her shoulder.

*I wouldn't grin yet,* Hannah thought. "Don't worry, Ebony," she whispered. "We're faster."

Uncle Joe, Hannah's trainer, patted Hannah's knee. "Just do your best."

Being the last rider had given Hannah time to

133

focus. Hours of practice now would be poured into seconds. Hundreds of times through the barrel run would be condensed to one time through. Hannah couldn't let Walt's accident stop her. She had sacrificed so much to get here. She just wished Papa could see her ride.

"And now, folks," the announcer said, "Megan Shibley of Clinton, Maine, on Butler!"

A gate clanged open. Hannah imagined the hooves pounding. She rode the race in her mind, as if it were her own.

"Hannah Parmenter?" Bob looked up from his clipboard. He nodded at Uncle Joe, then motioned to Hannah.

Hannah caught her breath. This was it! Heart pounding, she walked Ebony after the man.

"This is as far as I kin go," Uncle Joe chuckled. "You're on your own, honey."

Ebony's hooves followed Bob's boots to the orange chutes and starting gates. Hannah had seen countless rodeos on TV and had watched some live. Now she was in one—the Texas Mesquite Rodeo, Skowhegan State Fair, Maine.

Being back here was like being backstage at a play. You found out how things really work, and you had a part in what the audience saw. Hannah wanted this audience to see an upset by the last rider.

Bob shook Hannah's hand. "Good luck."

"Thanks." Hannah waited back away from the next rider. The roar of the crowd filled her head. It was inside her, in her heart. Now there was only one more rider before her. A gate to Hannah's left swung open, and a girl rode from the arena.

"18.2 for Megan Shibley, with two riders left!"

*Don't think about the others,* Hannah told herself. *Pretend Kennie's here, and you're racing her.*

"Adrianne Barrie of Cody, Wyoming, on Lightning!" The gate slammed open, and Lightning shot into the arena.

Hannah put her riding quirt in her teeth and walked Ebony ahead where Bob pointed. She leaned over Ebony's neck, whispering, "We're gonna do it, Ebony!"

The next gate opened, and Adrianne rode back.

"16.3 for Adrianne Barrie! Jesse Hawkins still leads!"

Hannah was poised in her saddle, her eyes on the gate.

"Now the deciding rider! Hannah Parmenter of Beaver Island, Maine, on Ebony!"

The gate slammed open. "Go! Go! Go!" Hannah yelled.

Ebony's power came alive. He shot toward the first barrel, neck forward. Ebony leaned to the right into the first corner, thrusting his front hooves to the left of his body, driving himself around the barrel. *Don't slip, Ebony.* They took the corner tight, in control.

*Now, Ebony, now! Rocket us out of here!*

With her left hand outstretched with the reins and her right hand pressing the saddle horn, Hannah held herself just above the saddle. Uncle Joe had taught her not to have her weight bouncing on Ebony's back, working against him.

Hannah was powerless, yet powerful because of Ebony. The night was inside her: the rides, the food vendors, the crowd, the lights, the arena, the barrels. She knew exactly where the barrels were, what Ebony would do next, what she needed to do. Hannah was living fully in these few seconds.

Approaching the second barrel, Hannah remembered Uncle Joe's direction: "Give him his head on the barrels!" Ebony had to slow for the corner, but he was like a river forced to flow through a narrow channel. When you let it go, the river rushes in its full Niagara.

"Hustle now! Hustle in between!" Hannah had heard Uncle Joe say many times. She focused her attention on the third barrel, anticipating Ebony's deep lean to the left. She guided Ebony's approach, careful not to overshoot it, to use the speed they built to drive them around it. Power under control, power focused on that loop around the barrel, that kind of power took Hannah's breath away.

The crowd was impressed, too, because Hannah heard them stomping on the bleachers.

Ebony shot out of the corner, straight for the finishing gate. *We're going home, Ebony!* Hannah now signaled Ebony with her quirt—faster, faster! As quickly as it began, it was over. Hannah reined Ebony in and rode out of the arena.

"HANNAH PARMENTER OF BEAVER ISLAND, MAINE ON EBONY..."

Hannah could not hear any more of the announcer's voice. The crowd roared, stomped, hooted. Did they cheer this long for everyone? What was her time? Hannah turned Ebony and rode toward the holding area.

A clown with red suspenders and green kneesocks shooed her back. That was when Hannah dared to believe it. "What...why?"

"Git that long-handled piece o' black lightnin' back out thar!"

Ebony's racehorse style returned just for a moment as he trotted in perfect majesty to center arena. Hannah stood in her stirrups. She grinned, waving her Stetson.

Mama leaned over the rail, forgetting Walt while she snapped picture after picture.

Hannah stared at the crowd, at all the faces all cheering. Aunt Theresa was yelling herself hoarse. Hannah had never before heard Auntie yell!

Hannah turned to see the rodeo master riding into the ring, holding a trophy and a long white envelope. Then she saw it: the lighted sign! Her time in the barrel race was 15.7, three-tenths of a second less than the next fastest contestant.

"I did it," she shouted into the din. "I did it!"

"Congratulations," the man said. Their horses stood side by side. "Ladies and gentlemen, Hannah Parmenter and Ebony are going to Dallas, Texas! Be sure to catch the Texas Mesquite Rodeo on national TV—two weeks from now!"

Once Hannah had escaped the news photographers, Uncle Joe drove her and Mama and Aunt Theresa to the hospital. All the way there and all the way up to Walt's room, Hannah kept re-riding the race, from the opening of the gate to her last view of the crowd.

But whatever had happened to Caylin? Her friend had missed the whole thing. Hannah had planned to stay at the fairgrounds until late, going on rides with Caylin. Instead, Caylin hadn't even shown up, and Walt was in the hospital. This wasn't how Hannah had pictured her rodeo win. *But I won,* she told herself.

"Papa *really* saw the whole thing on TV?" Hannah asked as they got on the elevator. Mama had called the hospital while Hannah was having her picture taken by the news photographers.

Mama laughed. "Like I told you, he saw it in the waiting room while the doctors worked on Walt's leg. By the time they announced you winner, the whole waiting room was cheering."

Still dressed in her rodeo clothes, Hannah held her trophy and certificate and the letter describing the prize trip to Dallas: entry into the competition, four airline tickets, and four rodeo tickets. They all stopped at room 227, and Mama stuck her head in. "It's us."

Walt lay on white sheets, his leg in a cast held up by ropes and pulleys. Mama went straight to Walt and sat in a chair by his bed.

Papa held out his arms. Hannah ran into them. "Our rodeo champ! Great ride, honey!" He hugged her.

"I did it, Papa! I didn't believe it until that clown wouldn't let me go."

"Congratulations, Han," Walt said. "Papa says you were awesome."

"Thanks. How you doing, Walt?" Hannah asked. "We were really freaked out when you fell."

"I'm all right. They gave me a bunch of pain-killer. I'm just mad I missed the whole rodeo." Walt forced a grin.

Uncle Joe took off his cowboy hat. "You kept a cool head to get away with only your leg hit."

"What exactly has the doctor said?" Mama asked.

"I'll be here a few days," Walt said. "It's a nasty break."

Papa looked around at everyone. "This day has had a lot of surprises."

Uncle Joe nodded. "Bad and good, *non?*"

"Certainly not boring," Walt said.

"And the excitement's not over yet." Hannah set her trophy down and opened her letter. "Now we get to go to Texas!"

No one said anything. Mama looked at Papa.

Uncle Joe looked at Hannah, his hat on his knee. "More rodeo?"

"What about the lodge?" Mama said. "We can't afford to pay the Sampsons to run it again. When you entered the rodeo, we hardly thought...I mean, we thought it would be an honor just to get you to compete."

"But it's my prize." Hannah looked around the room. "We *have* to go. Didn't you hear the rodeo master? The Texas Mesquite Rodeo's on national TV and everything. Kennie MacKenzie might even be racing, and I would race against her."

"We'll have to discuss it," Papa said.

"It doesn't look like I'll be going anywhere." Walt winced.

"It's two weeks away," Hannah said. "You'll be better by then."

"There's another surprise," Papa said. "Caylin had her tonsils out this morning. She's in a room down the hall."

"No way!" Hannah cried. "That means she can't perform tomorrow night! We thought the antibiotics would keep her well till after the pageant."

"She's running a fever," Papa said. "The doctors are working to bring it down."

"Poor girl," Aunt Theresa said. "She was so looking forward to the pageant."

"Could I go see her?" Hannah asked.

"She told us to make sure you come," Papa said. "Room 242."

When Hannah walked into the room, Caylin was alone. Her red hair was bright on the white bed, and a long tube ran from a bag of clear liquid to a needle in her arm.

"Hi, Hannah," Caylin whispered. "Congratulations. I saw you on TV."

"You did? Great! I wondered where you were." Hannah hadn't expected Caylin to look so pale, and Caylin's eyes were kind of puffy, too. "What's with the tube?"

"Intravenous fluids—IV, the nurse calls it." Caylin smiled weakly. "You can sit on my bed."

Hannah sat at the foot of the bed.

"They're pushing all the liquids..." Caylin stopped talking suddenly. She touched her throat, then pointed to a glass on the table.

"I'll bet your throat's really raw." Hannah passed Caylin the water.

"It's really sore," Caylin gasped.

"I'm sorry about the pageant," Hannah said.

"I know. I really wanted to be in it." Caylin's eyes dropped. She ran her hand over her sheet, smoothing it. "Has Mrs. Winters, the pageant lady, talked to you yet?"

"To me? Why?"

"The runner-up is out of town. Mrs. Winters was wondering what to do, and I...I suggested you could take my place. She"—Caylin took a sip of water—"she agreed. You couldn't win the trophy, but you'd represent Laketon."

"Me?" Hannah jumped up. "In the pageant? Do you think I can do it?" Hannah remembered the Miss Lakeland pageant. It had looked scary, but fun.

Caylin looked up from fiddling with the tape that held the IV needle in her arm. "I think you could. I suggested it, didn't I?"

"Does that hurt?" Hannah asked.

"The needle? Not really. So do you want to do the pageant?"

"Yeah, sure, why not? I've sung solos in church before—well, twice. It can't be that impossible."

Hannah imagined herself on stage. "Oh, Caylin, what should I sing?"

"Aunt Theresa practiced 'Clementine' with me. That's what I was going to sing."

"Yeah," Hannah said. She really did not want to sing "Clementine." "Maybe."

"You need to find Mrs. Winters, and"—Caylin wiped a tear from her cheek with the back of her hand and took a sip of water—"and tell her you'll do it."

"I'll do that," Hannah said. "I should go. It really hurts you to talk, doesn't it?"

Caylin nodded.

"I'd better go talk to Aunt Theresa, anyhow. I don't have much time." Hannah paused by the door. "Is the pageant on TV?"

Caylin nodded.

"Good. At least you can watch it. See you tomorrow?"

"Tomorrow," Caylin said, wiping away another tear.

# Chapter Sixteen

# Stage Fright

The fairgrounds were still quiet early Saturday. Hannah eyed the big outdoor stage with its huge grand piano. She and Aunt Theresa were checking out the pageant site. Mama and Papa had agreed that Hannah could perform, and Mrs. Winters was delighted.

The stage was much bigger than the one in Laketon High's gym, but that didn't scare Hannah. "Aunt Theresa, let's go to that music store in town. I need to pick out a song." Hannah stuck her hands into her sweatshirt pockets and sauntered toward the parking lot.

"I've practiced 'Clementine' already. I thought you'd sing that."

Hannah wrinkled her nose. "'Clementine's' silly, Auntie." She stopped walking and frowned at her aunt.

Aunt Theresa waved at the empty chairs in front of the stage. "Hannah, crowds make me nervous. Why, in Laketon it was all folks I know, and I was still nervous. It will not be a good idea for me to play a song I haven't practiced."

"Please, Auntie? I'll pick one we both know."

"Okay. We'll go to the music store." Aunt Theresa sighed. I'll meet you at your motel at ten o'clock. I need to find Uncle Joe in the horse barns and tell him we're taking the truck."

Hannah hugged Aunt Theresa. "I knew I could count on you."

Hannah ran down the midway and past the exhibition buildings. She crossed the street to Elmwood Motel.

Mama let her in their room. "Papa's gone to gas up the car, so I waited to tell you we're going to the hospital now. I'll leave the second room key with you."

"But Mama, I need your help to get ready for the pageant."

"Hannah, Papa and I need to look after Walt. That's our priority today."

"Can't just Papa go?"

"No, Hannah. But Papa and I will be back in time to watch you perform."

Hannah flopped down on a bed. "What am I going to wear tonight?"

"You'll have to wear what you have."

"Promise you'll be back?"

"Promise. Call us in Walt's room if you need to talk." Mama paused in the doorway. "And Hannah, you don't get to be Texas Mesquite Miss of Maine, even if you're the best of the show. Just do your best for Jesus—and for Caylin."

"Let's try it again," Aunt Theresa said.

The manager of the music store had given Hannah and Aunt Theresa permission to practice in a back room. Hannah had bought a copy of "My

Country 'Tis of Thee" by Samuel F. Smith. Since she
had sung it at church, she knew it pretty well, and
it was a familiar tune to Aunt Theresa, too.
Songwriter Smith was once president of a Christian
college just a few miles from the fairgrounds. So
Hannah knew that for many in the crowd this patri-
otic hymn was popular.

Aunt Theresa played an introduction, then nodded at Hannah.

"My country, 'tis of thee..." Hannah sang through
all four verses.

Aunt Theresa took off her reading glasses.
"That's a bit long, isn't it? Why don't you pick two
verses to sing—the first and last maybe?"

Hannah looked at her sheet music. "It *would* be
easier to remember just two verses."

"You don't have to *remember* them. You'll have
the words with you."

"No way," Hannah said. "Tonight I'm doing it by
heart. It would look silly to have a piece of paper up
there."

"You've had only one day to practice. I don't
think this is a good idea."

"Trust me," Hannah said. "I can do it."

"It's different in front of a crowd."

"I can handle it."

Aunt Theresa put her glasses back on. "Well,
let's get back to practicing."

Hannah leaned against a wall in the crowded
dressing room, too antsy to sit. She ran over the
words of "My Country 'Tis of Thee" in her head—
again. She knew the words perfectly. Nervous as a
chipmunk and wondering when Aunt Theresa would

get there, she crossed the room to a kitchen cart holding a silver water jug and crystal tumblers. The scents of the other girls' hand lotions and perfumes were a lot different from the mix of animals, leather, and dirt she was used to.

Hannah filled her glass and strolled back to watch the others. Most wore fancy dresses, some short and flouncy, others long and sleek. A dancer stood by a wall of mirrors at the back of the room stretching her legs. She wore a dramatic, silky red and gold jumpsuit with flaps of material that would twirl and fly when she danced.

Hannah had decided to wear her denim skirt and red Western shirt with her Stetson hat and hand-tooled boots. Now she felt strangely heavy as she watched the girl practice her steps, light as a feather.

*Thank goodness,* Hannah breathed, as Aunt Theresa hurried in wearing the simple navy blue dress she had planned to wear for Caylin's performance. Clutching her sheet music, Aunt Theresa made a beeline for Hannah. "How're you doing?"

"Fine," Hannah said. "I'm just tired of waiting."

"I think waiting is the hardest part. Oh, my, Hannah, the stands are just about full!"

"Really, Auntie?"

Mrs. Winters clapped her hands. "First act in five minutes. There will be one person onstage and another waiting in the wing. Watch my directions."

"We're fourth," Hannah said, leading Aunt Theresa backstage.

Aunt Theresa smoothed her dress. "I keep praying I won't be too nervous."

"We'll be fine," Hannah said. Aunt Theresa was making *Hannah* nervous.

A flute player was first, then a ballet dancer,

then a girl who had been studying words on a pretty sheet of pink paper.

Hannah tried to focus as she had before barrel racing, but instead she kept straining to hear what was happening onstage. Finally, she heard applause. The flute player came back into the room, and the darkhaired girl in front of Hannah left.

*What will I do when I get out there? Smile at the crowd?* Hannah hadn't thought about it before.

"My country 'tis of thee...Our fathers' God to thee..." As ballet music came faintly from the stage, these words played through Hannah's mind. Hannah felt calmed. *You can do this,* she told herself.

Again, they heard applause.

Aunt Theresa squeezed her hand. "This is it."

The ballet dancer came back, her eyes bright and face flushed. Mrs. Winters led Hannah and Aunt Theresa into the wing, just offstage. They could see the darkhaired girl in a long purple dress center stage, beautiful under the stage lights.

Hannah poked Aunt Theresa. A man in a tuxedo sat at the grand piano. *A tuxedo?* Hannah was startled. The man played a fancy introduction, and Hannah recognized the tune: "Beauty and the Beast." The girl had the pretty pink sheet of paper, but Hannah didn't see her look at it. The girl's voice soared, and Hannah imagined it floating out over the audience, enrapturing them.

"We can't compare ourselves to others," Aunt Theresa whispered, sensing Hannah's dismay. "Let's just do our best."

Hannah nodded.

Finally, as the last powerful notes of "Beauty and the Beast" and the audience's applause still hung in the air, a stagehand gave Hannah a microphone. "Now," the emcee cried, like he was announcing a star, "representing Laketon, HAN-NAHH PAR-MEN-TERRR!"

Hannah's heart pounded as she crossed the stage in her boots. It took forever to reach the center, as she imagined all those people staring at her.

The emcee's smile was huge. "Welcome!" he said. "Where are you from, Hannah?"

"Beaver Island—that's...uh...just across Moosehead Lake from Laketon." Hannah looked at him, then remembered she should be looking at the crowd, too. It was strange to look at people she really couldn't see.

"We've had a flutist, a ballet dancer, and a soloist so far. Why did you choose to sing for us, Hannah?"

"I love to sing." *What am I supposed to say—that I don't know how to play anything?* "I...I thought of bringing my horse Ebony with me and doing a little barrel racing, but I figured the stage wouldn't be equipped for that." Hannah giggled nervously.

The audience laughed, and the emcee laughed, too. "Well, let's hear your song." He walked out of Hannah's line of vision.

Hannah took a deep breath, let it out slowly, then took another breath, as Aunt Theresa played the introduction. Together, just like they were supposed to, they hit the first note.

Hannah sang, almost in shock that it was really her voice filling the night air. The bright stage lights blacked out much of the audience, and even those people she could see she didn't *really* see.

By the end of the first verse, Hannah felt in complete control. The night was magic. Just as they had practiced, Aunt Theresa was playing a fancier version of the song in an interlude between the verses.

This was the time for Hannah to prepare for the fourth verse. *'My country'*—no, no, no. Hannah's head began to pound. She wanted to run. The interlude was almost over, and she couldn't remember the fourth verse. *'My country.'* Oh, *why didn't I bring the words with me? 'My country'*... She imagined laughing faces all staring at her.

Aunt Theresa paused, then triumphantly struck the first notes of the song. Hannah's boots felt like cement, her Stetson a lead weight on her head.

She opened her mouth. "My country 'tis of thee / Sweet land of liberty..." Hannah's eyes were wide with horror. She was singing the first verse twice!

Aunt Theresa hesitated, then kept on playing. Hannah kept singing. What else could she do? She tried to tell herself that since she couldn't see the audience, she was invisible, but she knew better. Mechanically, the words came out, the last one finally. She bowed slightly, like she was supposed to do.

The crowd applauded. *Politeness,* Hannah thought. *Pity.*

Hannah hurried off the stage and passed the microphone to a stagehand. Mrs. Winters was talking to the next performer. "Good job," she murmured.

"Thanks." Hannah choked back her tears.

Aunt Theresa was right behind her. "What happened?"

"All I could think of was v-verse one. I-I couldn't remember."

Aunt Theresa put her arm around Hannah's shoulder. "Oh, Hannah, I'm sorry. But every person in that audience knows what it's like to make a mistake."

Hannah wiped her tears, stepping out of her aunt's embrace. "Well, no one needs to feel sorry for me."

"Don't be angry about it, Hannah."

"I'm not angry." Hannah straightened her Stetson, even though it was already straight. "Let's get out of here. I just did this dumb beauty pageant as a favor to Caylin. I ride in rodeos. I don't do beauty pageants."

# Chapter Seventeen

# Barreling Along

The last thing Hannah wanted to do after the pageant was go to the hospital. She dawdled, letting her parents hurry ahead into Walt's room, her boots stepping on every tile square down the hall—green, blue, gray; green, blue, gray.

Hannah toyed with the zipper on Walt's old jacket Mama had grabbed for her from the trunk of the car. She wished Mama had let her get her own jacket from the motel before they left. Hannah felt silly with the old blue and orange ski jacket over her nice denim skirt.

"Feel any pain?" Hannah heard Mama ask.

"Not too much," Walt said.

Hannah stopped outside Walt's door.

"And how are you, Caylin?" Papa asked.

*Great. Caylin's here with Walt, too.*

"Your parents gone for the night?" Papa added.

"Walt invited me to watch the pageant, so I told them they could go." Caylin spoke so softly Hannah had to strain to hear.

*So you messed up tonight. Big deal,* Hannah told

herself. *Last night you won barrel racing.* She slipped in and scooted around a little jog in the wall inside Walt's door.

Caylin sat in a reclining chair beside Walt's bed, wrapped in a cozy pink robe. Her IV pole stood beside her, and she was still pale.

"Here comes Miss A-mer-i-ca," Walt sang, spotting Hannah.

Caylin applauded.

"Leave me alone, Walt." Hannah's eyes burned, and she clamped her teeth on every word. "It's just a dumb beauty pageant. Who cares, anyway? You couldn't have done any better!"

Everyone went silent—Uncle Joe, Mama, everyone. Hannah's eyes met Caylin's. Caylin looked away.

"I can't believe you," Walt said.

Mama stood up and picked up her coat. "That is enough for today, Hannah. We need to go to the motel and unwind. Tomorrow's Sunday, and this family needs some rest. I want to get back to Laketon for evening church."

"Mama's right," Papa said. "We'll stop on our way home tomorrow, Walt. Mama or I will be back on Monday. You okay with that?"

"I'll be fine," Walt said. "I can always call."

It was fine with Hannah to go back to the motel. She was tired, so tired. Once they were back on Beaver Island she could forget the pageant and concentrate on getting to Texas.

"Come in." Hannah raised her head from where she lay on her bed on her stomach reading. After church she had changed into her pajamas.

The ride back from Skowhegan had been quiet. No one had said a word about the rodeo. For now, Ebony was at Uncle Joe's.

Mama came in with a handful of mail. "Gone for a few days and there's stacks of letters to sort," she chuckled.

"Any for me?" Hannah flopped over.

Mama flipped through the stack and pulled out a *Rodeo* magazine.

"Awesome," Hannah said.

Mama sat down on the edge of the bed.

Hannah rolled over to make room. "What's up?"

"We need to talk sensibly about Texas. Your brother's in the hospital. We don't have any way to get Ebony from Maine to Texas—a three-day drive. And we can't afford to pay the Sampsons to run the lodge again. I'm sorry, honey but we have some problems here."

"Mama, I know I can win!"

"Maybe you can, but that's not the issue."

"But I know I can."

Mama was quiet a moment. "The lesson here, Hannah, is that when things get too big for us to handle, we need to put them into God's hands."

Hannah sighed. "I know, Mama."

"You've been under a lot of stress. How about we just commit this to the Lord? You need some rest."

Hannah nodded.

"Lord, we bring these things before You right now," Mama prayed. "We're thankful we can put this into Your hands and that we can have peace in our hearts because You care for us. We know that in Your love You'll keep a hand on us as a family. You know what's best for us."

"Lord," Hannah prayed, "thank You for helping Ebony and me go this far, and I pray You'll take care of things that would keep us from Texas. I also thank You, God, that Walt wasn't hurt too bad and that Caylin's tonsil operation went okay."

"Amen."

"Amen."

"Don't stay up too late." Mama picked up the mail.

"I won't."

Mama paused by the door. "You need to let go of this in your heart, Hannah. There are more important things than winning a rodeo."

The distant jingle of the phone woke Hannah Monday morning. She pulled her covers tighter, but the smell of coffee and bacon was tempting.

"Skowhegan Police Department?" Mama's excited voice rose, then dropped.

*Skowhegan Police?* Hannah's feet hit the floor. She grabbed her robe and ran for the kitchen.

"This is your day, Hannah!" A grin spread across Mama's face. "There was a two-thousand-dollar reward for the capture of Hamstring Harvey. You and Walt get to split it."

"Yes!" Hannah shouted. "Yes!"

"Shh," Mama warned. "Our guests."

"I'm spending my thousand dollars to pay Uncle Joe to take Ebony to Texas!"

"That may be fine, Hannah, but Uncle Joe may have no intention of going to Texas. And remember we still have the lodge and Walt to consider. Dish yourself some scrambled eggs. I saved some of that fresh homemade bacon for you, too."

Just as Hannah sat down, the phone rang again.

"Beaver Lodge," Mama answered. "This is Sandy

Parmenter. Oh, hello, Doctor Rosignol. Uh-huh. Oh?!"

Hannah didn't like the look on Mama's face.

"Tomorrow? You're sure it's necessary? What time should we be there? All right. Thanks." Mama hung up.

"Is there a problem with Walt's leg?" Hannah asked.

"Doctor Rosignol wants to operate. I need to talk to your father."

"Operate!"

"He has to have pins put in his leg. Papa and I need to be there. I'll need you to help Aunt Theresa run the lodge for the day."

Mama walked out, leaving Hannah to eat. The morning sun beamed through the window behind Hannah, warming her back. Hannah stared at her eggs. "Thanks a lot, Walt," she muttered, her mouth full of egg. "There goes the rodeo."

Hannah was glad no one heard her. It wasn't really Walt's fault. He didn't want to break his leg. He would love to go to Texas, Hannah knew. But still, it made her angry. She *couldn't* give up the Texas rodeo this easily.

Hannah was helping Aunt Theresa wash the supper dishes when Mama and Papa came home from the hospital the next evening.

"How's Walt?" Aunt Theresa asked as she shook the dishpan suds from her fingers.

"He's fine," Papa said. "Home on Friday, most likely. Caylin went home this afternoon. And it sounds like her dad's found a job in Skowhegan."

"Really?" Hannah tossed her wet towel onto the

rack behind the wood-burning range. "I'm gonna call Caylin!"

"Better give them a chance to settle in at home," Mama advised. "Call her tomorrow." She took off her coat and sank into the kitchen rocker. "I'm so thankful Walt's surgery went so well," Mama said. "Theresa and Hannah, you can't imagine how I appreciate you girls taking care of things."

*Girls.* It made Hannah fairly buzz with pleasure to have Mama lump her and Aunt Theresa together like that. *Papa said I'm 'most a woman,* Hannah considered.

"Sandy, we've got a lot of things to be grateful for," Papa observed.

"We sure have," Mama agreed. "How was your schoolwork today, Hannah?"

Hannah carried a stack of plates to the cupboard before answering. "I got a lot done," she said truthfully. But she did not mention that she had made no progress on making up for work lost while practicing for the rodeo. Though Aunt Theresa had helped Hannah while she stayed in Laketon, Hannah had gotten a bit behind.

"I'm gonna need your help tomorrow, Mama," Hannah said. "I *need* to ride Ebony at the club soon's I get my schoolwork done."

"I guess I can spare you," Mama teased.

"Come in for pie before you ride." Aunt Theresa smiled at Hannah and gathered up her coat and purse. "I'm baking apple tomorrow—Wolf Rivers— your favorite."

"Good deal!" Hannah grinned.

"Your aunt sure takes care of you," Papa said.

"I try," Aunt Theresa laughed.

Mama put her coat back on and walked with Aunt Theresa to her boat.

Papa slipped off his shoes. "How about some hot chocolate?"

"Sounds good," Hannah agreed. She grabbed three mugs from the cupboard as Papa got out the milk. Hannah didn't know when they'd last had hot chocolate together.

"Why do I hafta write all these essay answers? Isn't there a multiple-choice test I can take?" Hannah grumped the next day.

"Hannah, history is important. Adults must know what's happened in the past to make decisions for the future. This way you really learn it."

"Mama, you've got a wise answer for everything," Hannah said, not half meaning it.

"The phone!" Mama caught it on the third ring. "It's Caylin—for you, Hannah. Time to quit your schoolwork for today, anyway."

"Daddy got the job in Skowhegan!" Caylin squealed. Then she coughed. "Ouch, my throat. I'm on major pain medication."

"Great." Hannah tried to sound excited, too, even though she didn't want Caylin to move to Skowhegan. She and Caylin had been best buddies since the Coulsons moved to Maine. "When do you...?"

"We're staying in Laketon." Caylin giggled, catching Hannah's disappointment. She coughed again. "Daddy'll commute."

"Cool! If you were here, I'd swing you around!"

"Not on Serena's dock again," Caylin chuckled. "Hey, how's Walt? I went home before he came out of recovery."

"He's great, I guess. He's supposed to come

home Friday. And guess what? We each get a thousand dollars for capturing that Hamstring Harvey crook. I want to use mine to have Uncle Joe take Ebony to Texas. Mama and Papa are bent outta shape over Walt and someone to watch the lodge, but I'm sure Walt will be better by then."

"You guys get all the breaks!"

"Can you picture it?" Hannah hardly heard Caylin's remark. "Me'n Ebony in Texas! But, hey, instead of talking on the phone, maybe I'll see you later. I'm coming into town to practice. Tell your dad congratulations. Bye."

When Hannah got to Aunt Theresa's, the apple pies were still warm, and Uncle Joe was home.

"I hear you got a thousand dollars," Uncle Joe said. He scooped vanilla ice cream onto their pie.

"Yeah—perfect timing! Thanks, Uncle Joe. Mmm! Great, Auntie."

Uncle Joe sat down at the table. "How's Walt?"

"Doin' great. I think he'll be able to go to Texas."

"You're going to the Dallas rodeo?" Aunt Theresa raised an eyebrow.

"I've got a plan," Hannah said. "I just need a little help." She hadn't really planned to ask, but it seemed to slip out. "I have this money. If I give it to Uncle Joe for gas and motels, and if you, Auntie, will watch the lodge for a couple of days, all we hafta do is get Walt set up, and we're on our way."

Uncle Joe stopped chewing and frowned.

Aunt Theresa wiped her mouth. "It's *more* than a couple o' days, dearie. Joe and I'll have to think about this one."

"Of course," Hannah said.

Hannah didn't stick around long after that. She was dying to ride Ebony. No one else was at the club. Hannah loved the quiet, the tall pines bordering the property. She bent over Ebony's neck, talking to him, looking out across the empty practice arena at the barrels, soaking in the warmth of the sun, shielding her eyes from its brightness.

The late afternoon sun hung low on the horizon. The lights of the indoor arena in Texas would be bright, too. In her mind, Hannah smelled popcorn, cinnamon-smothered elephant ears, hot dogs. She leaned low to Ebony's ear. "We can do this, big feller. We're gonna beat Kennie MacKenzie!"

Hannah heard the roar of the crowd and the crackle of the announcer's voice on the loud-speaker. "Now heads up folks, this is a team to watch—Hannah Parmenter and Ebony, all the way from Beaver Island, Maine!"

The gate swung open. Hannah spurred Ebony, who flew like a dream. She rode each corner as if she were part of him, and the crowd cheered and hollered. When they rounded the third corner, the crowd began to stomp. With her quirt, she signaled Ebony full-speed for the stretch home, but he was so fast that she didn't need to bother. Waving to the crowd, Hannah trotted Ebony from the arena, his breathing powerful, his nostrils flaring. "I told you we could do it, boy!" Hannah whispered.

The clip-clop of a pair of chestnut quarter horses emerging from a woods trail startled Hannah. "Beat you to the stables!" a boy shouted to a girl who rode with him—and Hannah was back in Maine. Texas had vanished. It didn't matter. Soon, she expected, she'd really be there.

Mama and Papa were working in front of Beaver Lodge building a rock wall around a flower garden when Hannah cruised up to the dock. "Hi, Mama! Hi, Papa!" Hannah called. She hoped dinner was about ready. Her stomach was growling.

"How was your ride?" Papa set another bucket of rocks down beside Mama, who knelt next to a strip of black plastic that would keep the weeds down until the tulips grew in the spring.

"Great! I told Uncle Joe and Aunt Theresa about my idea to pay Uncle Joe to bring Ebony to Texas and have Aunt Theresa stay at the lodge. They're probably going to do it. They'll let us know."

"You asked them *what?*" Mama said. "Don't you think they've done enough for you already?"

"Hannah, I can't believe you did that." Papa wiped his forehead with his sleeve. He turned over a plastic bucket and sat on it.

"Aren't you forgetting Walt?" Mama asked.

"Walt's coming home Friday. You said so yourself."

"That doesn't mean he's going anywhere."

"He can stay with Aunt Theresa." Hannah forced a small smile.

"It won't be that simple," Papa said.

Mama went back to placing the rocks on the plastic. "I'll call Theresa in the morning and sort this out. You, Hannah, please check the casseroles in the oven and make us a big green salad. I don't want to hear any more about this rodeo until Papa or I bring it up."

"Yes, Mama." Hannah clomped up the porch steps in her new riding boots. *Can't Mama and Papa see how important it is for us to go to Texas? Maybe if I wait until Walt gets home, he'll help me convince them.*

# Chapter Eighteen

# Stuck-Up

"Mama, they're home!" Hannah spotted the boat way out in the lake. She had been doing schoolwork, but she kept checking the window every few minutes. Papa had left early Friday morning to pick up Walt from the hospital.

Mama came to the window. "Wonderful! And I've just finished serving the guests." She stepped out onto the porch.

Hannah followed in her socks. Mama had made Walt's favorite lunch—spaghetti.

Hunter danced on his chain, whimpering. Hannah unhooked him to let him race to the dock.

"I'm glad they're early," Hannah said. "I need to ride Ebony right after we eat."

Hunter pranced down to the water and back to Hannah with his ears alert and tongue hanging out. Hannah laughed and scratched his floppy ears.

"I talked to your Aunt Theresa," Mama said, as she and Hannah hurried toward the dock.

"Oh?" Mama hadn't said a word about the rodeo for days.

"I wanted to make sure they didn't feel pressured to do it. Papa and I certainly weren't expecting them to do such a big thing."

"What did Auntie say?"

"I was surprised," Mama said cautiously. "Despite your being so presumptuous, they've decided they want to do it."

"I knew they would! They won't be sorry. Ebony and I are going to win. You're all going to be so proud."

"Not so fast," Mama warned. "Walt is in no shape to travel."

Hunter raced out onto the dock, barking his silly head off. Walt sat with his cast propped up, waving and grinning. You'd think he hadn't seen Beaver Island or Mama or Hannah or Hunter for years.

As the boat neared the dock, Hunter bounded into it. He put his front legs on Walt and licked him and nuzzled him.

"Pesky mutt," Walt laughed and scratched Hunter's ears.

Papa tied the boat up and handed Walt his crutches. "Watch how well Walt can use these things."

Walt came down the dock on one leg, swinging along on the crutches.

Hannah nudged Mama. "See. He can go to Texas."

"Please—just let your brother come home!"

Walt laughed. "Hi, Mama."

Mama hugged Walt. "Welcome home."

"Thanks. Hi, Han."

"Hi."

"Whatcha got cookin', Mama? I'm tired of that hospital stuff."

"Boys!" Hannah laughed. "First thing they think about is food."

"You came at the right time," Mama said. "I made spaghetti—with moose venison meatballs."

Spaghetti was certainly Walt's favorite. Hannah got up twice to get her brother more, since he couldn't use his crutches and carry a plate. Walt scooted his chair back and reached for his crutches.

"Can I get you more?" Mama asked. "They must have starved you."

"I'll make it fine," Walt chuckled. "I just want more of that garlic bread." He crossed the kitchen expertly.

"See, Mama, Walt *can* go to Texas. He's eating like a horse."

"You talking about me?"

"Sure am."

"How do you think he's going to fly on the plane in those tiny seats?" Mama worried.

"Hey," Walt said, "I'm not staying here while you guys go to Dallas!"

"Great!" Hannah grinned.

"Hannah," Mama warned.

"Please?" Hannah looked from Mama to Papa.

Walt sat back down. "I do want to go. Why not just call my doctor—he'll okay it."

"It wouldn't hurt to call," Papa agreed.

Hannah slapped the table. "YES!"

"Hold your horses, young lady," Mama cautioned. "Don't get your hopes up. I'll call Doctor Rosignol. If he okays it, I'll check with the airline about Walt's cast."

"Well, if you'll excuse me, I'm going to practice with Ebony." Hannah carried her dishes to the sink.

Hannah ran up the lodge's front steps, full of adrenalin from a fabulous ride. She burst into the kitchen door, then braked, remembering how Mama had said not to get her hopes up. How could she not get her hopes up? She could hear Mama and Papa talking in the living room. She pulled her boots off on the doormat, then padded across the kitchen.

"Come in here, Hannah," Papa called.

Hannah sat on the couch, trying to read Mama's and Papa's faces.

"Walt's doctor says okay," Papa said. "The airline says since the Mesquite rodeo is paying for first-class tickets, Walt will have plenty of room for his cast."

"Yes!" Hannah squealed.

"And," Mama put in, "Sam Sampson will help Aunt Theresa with the chores, so Papa and I can go."

"YES! YES! YES!" Hannah leaped up and gave Mama and Papa each a bear hug.

"Careful you don't go through the ceiling," Papa laughed.

Hannah went straight to the kitchen to call Caylin.

"Guess what?" Caylin said as soon as she heard. "Now that my throat's better, my parents are planning a vacation before Daddy starts work. They want to drive southwest—clear to the Gulf of Mexico."

"TEXAS?!"

"Don't freak out, Han," Caylin laughed. "We can stop in Dallas for the Mesquite rodeo, now that you're in it."

"Dallas, here we come!" Hannah whooped.

"Wow!" Hannah said. The city of Dallas, far, far below in the morning mist, swam lazily past the window of the revolving restaurant.

"Cool!" Caylin cried. "This place is even bigger'n Hartford, Connecticut, where I used to live!"

"It takes your breath away, doesn't it," Mama murmured.

"We could use one of these tower restaurants on top of Bald Hill," Papa chuckled. "You could see the whole Allagash wilderness from Beaver Island."

"Roger and I are glad we could be here to see Hannah ride," Mrs. Coulson said.

"Glad for you, too, my little redheaded sweetheart." Mr. Coulson, whose hair was as red as Caylin's, patted his daughter's head.

"I'm so glad you got these restaurant reservations, Roger," Mama said. "Great idea."

As they ate breakfast atop Reunion Tower in downtown Dallas, Hannah, Walt, Mama, Papa, and the Coulsons watched the twin cities of Dallas and Fort Worth stretch into the distance. The Parmenters had arrived at the hotel the evening before, driving a minivan they'd rented at the airport that allowed room for Walt's cast. The Coulsons, already at the hotel, had arranged for them to eat together. Uncle Joe had called their room from his motel in Oklahoma, and he would arrive at the Mesquite rodeo arena later that morning.

Hannah glanced out the windows that stretched around the circular dining room. *Wow* was just about the only word that described this part of Texas.

"Where are the buffaloes and cowboys and cattle ranches?" Caylin asked.

"West of here," Mama said. "Since this restaurant is turning, I'm not sure which way west is."

"We drove from the west when we came into Dallas from the Dallas-Fort Worth Airport yesterday," Papa said. "I sure didn't see any buffaloes or cowboys, either. Plenty of cars, trucks, and skyscrapers, like New York, though." Driving in a city larger than Skowhegan, Maine, made Papa nervous.

"We saw two cowboys in the hotel this morning," Walt said. "They wore suits with fancy stitching, and they had on ten-gallon hats and riding boots."

"Fake cowboys!" Caylin wrinkled her cute nose. "Cowboys don't wear suits."

"Some cowboys in this town really do wear suits, Caylin," Mrs. Coulson explained. "It's not like the old Western movies they show on TV."

"Hey," Walt said. "Isn't that Kennie, the champion from Uncle Joe's videos?"

"Here? Where?" Hannah twisted in her seat.

"Really?" Caylin said, turning around, too.

Sure enough. There was Kennie MacKenzie, sitting three tables behind them, eating a strawberry waffle. Hannah had hoped she would get to compete against Kennie, and it sure looked like she might.

Hannah grinned at Walt. "She's the one I'm gonna beat tonight!"

Walt rolled his eyes. "'She's the one I'm gonna beat tonight,'" he mimicked. "Why do you have to be so stuck-up about this? Kennie's a *professional* rider."

"What do you know about competing in rodeos? At least I didn't get busted up jumping on a dumb steer. I won, remember?"

Caylin started busily eating. Mama and Mrs. Coulson stopped talking.

"Hannah Joy, that's enough!" Mama said.

"Yes, Mama."

Walt pursed his lips and stared out the window.

Hannah quietly finished eating. Then she unfolded a city map of Dallas she had bought in the hotel lobby. "This cost $4.95—can you believe it? In Laketon, they give free maps to the tourists."

"So, do we go out in the country for the rodeo?" Caylin asked.

"Doesn't look like it," Hannah said. "I'd like it better if the rodeo were out on the range, like in the old days of cattle drives and Texas longhorns. But we don't even leave this big city. Look here."

Caylin and Hannah bent over the map.

"From our hotel in downtown Dallas, we'll take the Thornton Freeway," Hannah explained. She was usually the family navigator when Mama drove to Augusta, Maine, or even to Boston. "That takes us to the President Lyndon B. Johnson Freeway, which goes south to Mesquite. See—here it says, 'Mesquite Championship Rodeo.'" Hannah placed her finger on a small red dot on the map.

"So we do get out of the city?" Papa asked. He had been talking with Mr. Coulson while the others studied the map.

"Not exactly," Hannah giggled. "Mesquite is a city, too. It's all part of metropolitan Dallas. So I guess it's a suburb."

"It sure is," Mama agreed, noticing that the map showed mostly dark yellow, designating city.

Papa studied the breakfast bill. "We need to raise our prices for meals at Beaver Lodge," he joked. He turned to Hannah. "Shouldn't we get on over to the rodeo arena?"

"Yeah. We gotta be there to meet Uncle Joe and Ebony. And I want to walk Ebony in the arena. It'll be a strange place for him.

"Not only for him." Papa raised an eyebrow. "I guess there won't be much time for sightseeing."

"Why doesn't Walt come with us, then?" Mr. Coulson suggested. "We plan to tour a bit—see where President Kennedy was shot—that sort of thing. He can stretch his leg across the backseat."

"I can hold his foot." Caylin snickered and made a face.

"There's a devoted friend," Mama laughed.

Walt grinned at Mama and Papa.

"It would be perfect if Walt wants to," Mama said. "Harry and Hannah and I could get what we need from the hotel and head straight to Mesquite."

"Fine," Papa said. "I may lose my breakfast if I have to drive in this traffic, though."

"I can drive, Harry," Mama suggested.

"If we could just rent a horse and wagon...." He shrugged, then laughed. "Sandy, you've driven in Boston. If you want to try wheelin' through Dallas, I'll ride shotgun and pray."

# Chapter Nineteen

# The Showdown

"This is it, Ebony," Hannah whispered as she led Ebony by the bridle around the empty arena. Later, the stands would be full of stomping, shouting people. For now it was just the two of them, besides a janitor sweeping with a push broom.

Hannah kicked at the dirt. The earth was softer and deeper than at home. "Don't let this dirt bother you, Ebony," she said. "We're gonna do great. I can *feel* it." Hannah tried to keep a soothing tone to calm Ebony, but her excitement got the better of her. She ran her hand down Ebony's powerful neck. "Don't let this place make you nervous. If we want to win, we gotta keep our heads."

The building was grander than Hannah had imagined. It was strange to be in it alone, with the empty stands rising eerily all around. The shades were down along the vendor counters, and the dark scoreboard added to the spookiness.

Hannah's mind raced again and again past the starting gate slamming open in front of her, the announcer narrating her every move, the blaze of lights, the blurred colors of the crowd, the mingled smells of animal and popcorn—she and Ebony in perfect control. *Winners.* "Just wait till tonight, Ebony," Hannah said aloud. "This place will be popping. You and I are gonna *rule!*"

Hannah rode Ebony from the arena, back toward the holding pens behind the chutes and stands. She rode past the walk leading to the pen for bulls. Being behind the scenes made her feel powerful. She was now an insider, a competitor, like the hundreds of cowboys and cowgirls who had competed here before her.

Hannah was bursting to know what time the scoreboard would show for her. Her fastest time in practice was 15.5 seconds. That was all she needed tonight. "One good run, big boy!" Ebony's hooves echoed on the concrete floor. The narrow walk, like a tunnel with no ceiling, made Hannah claustrophobic. Back here were the stalls where the barrel racers kept their horses. Hannah watched as riders and their trainers busily led their steeds from their horse trailers.

"She will be a big rodeo, *non?*" chuckled Uncle Joe, holding the gate as Hannah led Ebony into his stall.

"Bigger'n I could imagine," Hannah giggled.

"You're Hannah's trainer, Mr. Boudreau?" A rodeo worker stepped up to Uncle Joe.

"Sure am."

"Your truck's in the way, sir. You'll need to move it."

"Sorry. I'll be right out." Uncle Joe turned to Hannah. "You'll be okay alone while I move ze truck an' trailer?" He shot a loving glance at his niece.

"I'm fine, Uncle," Hannah laughed. "Or should I say 'coach'?" To tell the truth, Hannah partly wanted to be alone. This was *her* rodeo. Deep inside, though, Hannah felt she needed Uncle Joe to encourage her until she and Ebony raced.

The rodeo announcer's voice crackled over the loudspeaker: "Miss Texas will lead us in the national anthem."

*Wow!* Hannah remembered, *Miss Texas was the runner-up in the Miss America contest!*

The afternoon with Uncle Joe had evaporated into the clouds.

"Now our first calf roper of the evening, Bill Peterson, of Tulsa, Oklahoma!" A buzzer sounded. Hannah knew this meant the calf roper was out of the chute on his horse, chasing down the calf. He would rope it, jump off his horse, flip the calf on its back, tie its legs together, and hold his hands up to signal he was finished.

Hannah eyed Kennie MacKenzie across the holding area talking to her parents. She could hardly believe people would be watching her and Kennie on national TV in the *same* race. Hannah grinned. Though she looked controlled on the out-side, on the inside she kicked up her heels like a bucking bronco. She and Ebony were going to *fly!*

Hannah led Ebony out of his stall, past the other contestants. The staging areas were a jumble of bulls and broncos, boots and Western shirts, a maze of people, all with their races to win, their bulls to ride, their steers to wrestle.

Barrel racing was next, and Hannah would ride seventh out of fifteen. The first two barrel racers had been called out to position themselves by the chutes and gates into the arena.

As Hannah checked Ebony's saddle, she turned the cloverleaf over in her mind, envisioning, feeling Ebony run full speed on the straightaways, holding back around the barrels. She sighted their course—faster, faster, in perfect control. *God, help us keep control, help us on the third barrel, I know I can do this. Don't panic, Hannah Parmenter. You are prepared.*

Caylin and Walt were almost to her when she saw them. Caylin waved. She wore a soft, pretty green sweater Hannah hadn't seen before, and her red curls spilled over her shoulders. She carried a yellow rose. *Doesn't she know this is a rodeo, not a beauty contest?* Hannah wondered.

Walt picked his way through the riders and horses on his crutches. He wore his red and black Western shirt, cut-legged jeans over his cast, and boots—well, one boot. "Hi," Walt said. "We were hoping we'd find you."

"Hi," Hannah said. "Are you guys supposed to be here? I thought you were sitting in the bleachers already."

"We came to tell you, 'Break a leg,'" Walt laughed.

"Thanks a lot," Hannah said, eyeing his plaster cast.

Caylin scanned the room. "Everyone else has a helper back here," she said.

"Yeah, I don't know what's happened to Uncle Joe." Hannah shrugged. "If he wants to sit in the bleachers, I can concentrate better by myself, any-way."

Caylin held out the rose. "A yellow rose of Texas—like in the song. I bought you this for good luck."

"Thanks, but I don't need luck," Hannah said. "With barrel racing, it's skill—a matter of who's the fastest, and I'm ready. It's not like a beauty pageant, where it's all opinion and anyone could win. Thanks anyway." Hannah made no move to take the rose.

Caylin froze, her hand still outstretched.

Walt moved closer to Hannah on his crutches, his eyes flashing fire. "You've got an attitude, kid— a real bad attitude, Hannah Joy Parmenter! I don't care whether you win this race or come in last. You're a loser." Walt spoke in a low, strained voice, like he was trying not to shout. "Uncle Joe cleaned out his garage, bought you a membership in the riding club, drove Ebony around the lake, practiced with you every..."

"What...?" Hannah sputtered. *What does all this have to do with anything?* she thought. *Why doesn't Caylin defend me?*

"Just listen for once," Walt snapped. His blue eyes locked on her emerald ones. "Uncle Joe drove Ebony all the way here, and Aunt Theresa stayed behind to run Beaver Lodge. Mama and Papa have been helping you with everything—'Yes, Hannah' this and 'Yes, Hannah' that; 'As soon as we can, Hannah.' It's never fast enough for you," Walt whispered hoarsely. "'I'm going to win the rodeo, I'm going to win the rodeo,'" he singsonged. "Well, you never would have won the first one without everybody's help.

"We were so busy at the lodge, I don't know why we bothered," Walt went on. "You don't appreciate anything. I don't think I've heard you say thank you even once. You act like we owe you all this. Well, we don't, and I'm never doing another chore for you again.

"And Caylin—you walked all over her and the pageant. You never considered how disappointed she was and how hard it was for her to ask you to take her place. All you ever think about is yourself. 'I'm a rodeo rider. I don't do dumb beauty pageants,'" Walt mimicked.

Caylin's eyes were fixed, not focusing, filled with tears.

"Caylin's *my* friend, too," Walt said. "I won't let you treat her this way. Come on, Caylin, let's go!" Walt gripped his crutches. "If you think you got to this rodeo alone, go ahead and see how you like *alone.*"

"I have to go," Caylin mumbled. She followed Walt toward the arena.

Hannah stared after them. She closed her eyes and willed her spinning thoughts to stop. *You're a loser, Hannah. No—stop! Stop! Stop! Stop! How could Walt do this to me right before the race? If I lose, it'll be his fault.*

A buzzer sounded. Hannah's eyes snapped open. A gate clanged open.

*The first rider.* Hannah had missed the introduction of the first barrel rider. *Is Walt right? Have I been missing something all along? No! Stop! How dare Walt try to ruin my race just because he broke his leg! He's jealous. Caylin, too. She's disappointed because she missed her big chance at the fair pageant.*

The crowd was quiet, waiting the first rider's time.

"17.7 for Annalisa Taylor!" the announcer's voice rang.

"Only 17.7?" Hannah whispered. "We can beat that, Ebony!"

The buzzer sounded again, and the gate clanged open.

"Riders three and four, follow me. The rest of you be ready." It was Jennifer, the woman in charge of coordinating the barrel racers.

Hannah watched the two girls ride down the cement corridor. One of them twisted around in her saddle, and a man across the room waved her a thumbs-up. He reminded Hannah of Uncle Joe with his woodsy flannel shirt and beard.

Hannah rested her forehead on Ebony's neck. Ready? She'd never been less ready.

*Concentrate, Hannah! Your turn's gonna come fast.*

*I don't care if you win, you're a loser.* Walt's words came back like a flood. *Stop! Stop!* Hannah screamed in her head. *I won't let them ruin this!*

Hannah mounted Ebony and settled into her saddle. *Pay attention. Ride to win.* One by one, riders left, buzzers sounded, scores were announced, and the riders rode back into the pens. Hannah willed herself to concentrate, to listen.

17.7. 17.5. 16.7 17.0. 17.9. Hannah reviewed the scores. Why wasn't she more excited? These riders were in a slump. Hannah knew she could do as well as 15.5.

Jennifer held up her clipboard. "Riders seven and eight, follow me."

Sitting tall in her saddle, Hannah followed Jennifer's swinging ponytail. Ebony's hooves clopped on the concrete, echoing Walt's words: *See how you like alone, like alone.* And Hannah was feeling very alone.

The crowd groaned. Rider six had tipped a barrel.

Hannah followed Jennifer along the back of the chutes to the gates. Jennifer nodded at her and pointed to a spot about ten feet back.

Hannah waited, sitting solidly on Ebony. Hearing the crowd up close almost distracted her from Walt. *Almost.* She tried to keep alert for directions. Hannah tried to go over everything she was going to need as she rode. She sensed Ebony's excitement, and she took some comfort in knowing at least one of them was ready.

The gatekeeper opened the gate, and the girl who'd knocked the barrel over rode through and back the way Hannah had come. The gate closed, and the gatekeeper motioned Hannah closer.

Ebony stepped up to the steel gate. Hannah eyed the traffic light by the gate into the arena. It was red, then yellow. The clock high above the arena said 00.00.

Hannah clenched her leather riding quirt in her teeth. This was it!

# Chapter Twenty

# An Old Family Story

The loudspeaker crackled: "22 seconds with penalty for Rebecca Sorenson. And now, Hannah Parmenter, all the way from Beaver Island, Maine!"

The buzzer sounded, the gate swung open, and the light turned green. Hannah spurred Ebony with her heels. As his huge body lunged out of the gate, she felt them enter a shrunken world where each second was an hour. Except for her and Ebony and the ground beneath them, the arena no longer existed. She was aware only of the thump of Ebony's hooves striking the dirt, mocking her, drumming to the time of Walt's words: *You're a loser. You're a loser. You're a loser.*

Hannah knew she should be concentrating, but her mind was full of Ebony's black neck stretched forward, full of the brown dirt, and the thumping of his hooves, steady as a drum being thumped with the palm of a hand. *You're a loser. You're a loser. You're a loser.*

Ebony's weight shifted. As the horse slowed and

176

leaned low to the right around the first barrel, Hannah watched how his black ears pointed forward, saw the braided brown leather bridle around the back of his head. Ebony's head had been all she could see when she and Papa had led Ebony across the channel to the mainland. While Papa paddled, Hannah had held Ebony's reins. Ebony swam alongside, his black fur shiny and wet, the leather of the bridle darkened by the water. Fall sunshine spilled from a blue, cloudless sky to make the vast expanse of Moosehead Lake shimmer, its surface rippling bright over its mysterious blue depths.

Hannah remembered how Ebony's neck rose out of the water when his feet found the bottom at the far side of the channel. His mane drifted up, then his nostrils widened, and he snorted and reared and bolted back into the deep water, tipping the canoe over and ripping the reins from Hannah's hands. Hannah had lunged for the reins, but Papa was ahead of her, already swimming hard after Ebony.

Hannah remembered Papa swimming back, saw him standing up to his chest in water, soaking wet. Ebony bolted into Beaver Island's woods and headed for home. Papa told her not to worry, that they would try again.

"When?" Hannah heard herself demanding. "Today? Tomorrow?"

Hannah saw herself pouting as Papa promised to do his best to get away from his work with the tourists. "I'll do it as soon as I can, honey," he said. "But it might be several days before I can take time off again."

Hannah saw the anger on her own face as she blurted out, "You don't know how important this is! You don't even care!"

She saw Papa stop mid-stroke, his paddle hanging into the water, his warm gray eyes hurt. "Hannah, I wouldn't be here if I didn't care. Should I send the tourists home? We have bills to pay."

Hannah hadn't answered him, and now his words played over and over in her head.

"I already rescheduled things today," Papa had said. "You know I have tour groups to guide and chores at the lodge."

*Chores at the lodge.* Hannah recalled how she had sat on Aunt Theresa's old oak chair, her plate full of ham, green beans, and mashed potatoes. Auntie was smiling across the table at her. "I talked to your mom today, Hannah. They have a lot of guests, just about a record for this time of year—can you believe it? But everything's going well. Even Walt's got a sense of humor about doing your chores."

Hannah felt horribly off balance, and it wasn't just Ebony's deep lean to the left as he came into the second barrel. Hannah's right hand held the saddle horn tightly, tighter than it needed to be held.

"Your family wants you to have a good shot at this rodeo," she heard Aunt Theresa say. She pictured Mama milking Molly, Walt hauling firewood into the living room and cleaning guest rooms, Mama cooking all the meals, serving the guests, doing all the dishes while she, Hannah, stayed in Laketon to practice.

Hannah had never before been aware of the pressure on her feet in her stirrups as Ebony leaned, or that she could hear every single thump of Ebony's powerful hooves. She had never noticed how the hair of his mane floated between strides coming around a corner, how he snorted as he breathed, or how close he ran to the barrels. The big barrel was only inches from Hannah as she leaned with Ebony, his powerful hind legs driving them out of the turn.

With the pounding of his hooves, Hannah heard again, *You're a loser. You're a loser. You're a loser.* She saw Caylin as Walt said it. Caylin stood in the holding area in her green sweater, her hand extended holding the yellow rose, the rose Hannah had never taken from her hand. The look on Caylin's face was the same look she had had in Walt's hospital room when Hannah called the whole pageant stupid. Hannah saw Caylin's pretty face as she hadn't seen it before: wide-eyed disbelief, as though it had been slapped, a face that betrayed the hurt her silence tried to hide.

Hannah saw Caylin's red curls splayed messily about her white hospital pillow as Caylin struggled to ask her to be in the pageant. Caylin's eyes were puffy then. Hannah had assumed at the time that Caylin's tears were caused by her sore throat, but now she knew that wasn't true. Caylin was upset about the pageant.

It would have hurt Hannah horribly to miss the barrel race, and it would have hurt even more to ask someone else to take her place. But strangely, since the starting gate slammed open, rodeos didn't seem all that important anymore. What was really hurting Hannah was how she had treated the people who loved her most.

Hannah felt Ebony's weight shift as he leaned into the third barrel. Despite Ebony's wild lunge forward coming out of the turn, he was captive to Hannah's slow-motion world. Hannah heard her stirrups slapping against Ebony's sides. She smelled sweating horsehide on her saddle, on herself, coming up off Ebony's powerful neck.

Hannah took her riding quirt from between her teeth with her right hand and signaled Ebony full speed ahead for the long stretch home. The supple leather handle of the small riding whip brought an image of Uncle Joe putting it into her hand for the first time. It had been cloudy that day and colder than usual, but Uncle Joe was at the riding club, as always, in his woodsy flannel shirt and old Northwoods Logging Company jacket.

"You can't win a race on yesterday," Uncle Joe always said. Hannah heard him cheering her, not caring who else was at the club to hear, saw him jumping up and down the first time she got 15.5. She saw laughter in his eyes when he said, "I just heard Rome really *was* built in a day. Keep your perspective. Remember the important things." And she saw herself scowl at him.

Hannah now saw nothing but the tall green gate rising in front of her. She hoped Uncle Joe was cheering now.

The gate swung away from her, and she trotted through, past the next two riders, back toward the holding area and the stalls.

"For this young rider, 16.6," the announcer said, "a new lead score by a tenth of a second, with eight more gals yet to ride!"

"Great job!" Jennifer said. All eyes were on Hannah as she rode in. "You're in first place!"

Hannah only nodded, fighting tears. It hadn't really been a great job, she knew.

Jennifer called for riders ten and eleven. Hannah let Ebony walk around as some of the others who had already raced were doing. She heard and saw, but not really. It was like when she was on stage at the pageant, and her eyes saw people in the front row, but she didn't really *see* them individually.

Now all Hannah could see was Caylin with her red curls, confused and hurt, holding out the rose. Angry Caylin climbing out of the cold water after Hannah had pulled her in.

Hannah felt her stomach knot.

Another buzzer went off. A boy in a Stetson hat like Walt's gave a returning rider a high five. The girl leaned down in her saddle, and Hannah noticed wisps of scarlet curls, red as Caylin's, tumble from beneath the girl's hat.

In her mind, Hannah felt Mama's arms around her, saw her sitting on her bed in the dark, talking, the moon coming through the window. Somewhere in the room, a man laughed, full, happy, jolly—just like Papa.

Hannah felt a great sob rise in her throat. She swung off Ebony, her boots landing solidly on the sawdust-covered concrete. Quickly, she closed Ebony in his stall and strode to the holding area's back door. Somewhere out there were Mama and Papa.

"Hey," Jennifer called. "The event isn't over yet." She stopped Hannah. "You're in first place, or you may win second or third. You're not supposed to leave."

"I n-need to leave," Hannah said. "I have something more important than this rodeo to deal with."

Hannah felt the sob pushing on her insides, growing, rising, struggling to escape. She pushed the door open and ran. She ran down the hall toward the stairs to the grandstand. She *had* to find her family.

She heard a voice. Papa's? Was she imagining? Hannah rounded the corner to where the hall spilled into the food and souvenir stands—right into Papa, Mama, and Uncle Joe.

"Hannah!" Mama exclaimed. "Where are you going?"

"To find you."

Papa squeezed Hannah. "Great ride!"

Hannah buried her head in his soft flannel shirt.

Papa held her. "I'm sorry about your time. Riders nine and ten were lightning."

"Did they beat me?"

"I thought you knew." Papa was silent a second. "Hannah, what's the matter?"

Hannah hugged him harder. "I'm so sorry," she sobbed. "I'm so sorry." Her shoulders shook.

"Sorry for what, honey?"

"Everything. Walt was right about everything."

Hannah pulled back from Papa and wiped her eyes with her sleeve. Puzzled, Papa, Mama, and Uncle Joe looked at one another.

Hannah struggled to put into words what the vivid pictures that had reeled through her mind during the race had said so clearly. "Everybody's worked to get me here, and I haven't appreciated it. All...all I've thought about is myself."

"Do you want to talk about it?" Papa asked softly.

Hannah nodded, glad for Papa's arm around her shoulder, glad for Mama fishing in her purse to get her a tissue, glad for Uncle Joe, who would forgive her almost before she asked.

Hannah spotted Walt and Caylin making their way through the crowd. She nodded in their direction. "Do you guys mind waiting? I really need to talk to them."

"Go ahead," Mama said. "You know where to find us."

Caylin was still holding the yellow rose. Did Hannah dare hope?

❊ ❊ ❊ ❊ ❊ ❊ ❊

Hannah hunkered down into the fringed buckskin jacket Papa had bought her in Texas, careful not to squish the yellow rose on her lap. She pushed into Mama's side and let Mama hug her to warm them both. "I guess this must be how Kennie MacKenzie feels about getting back to Wyoming," Hannah said. Kennie had won the barrel race, for the second year in a row. Hannah came in fourth— ahead of eleven of the fifteen contestants—but one place too low for a prize.

Hannah peered past Papa, who steered the big motorboat. The copper roof of Beaver Lodge gleamed in the afternoon sun among the majestic green pines and slender white birches. Bald Hill rose behind the lodge, its thatch of blueberry bushes now red with their fall leaves. Hannah was glad to be home.

Aunt Theresa met them at the door. "How are all the travelers? Here, let me get that." She took a plastic sack that was slipping from Hannah's arms as Hannah concentrated on keeping her yellow rose safe. "Letting them do all the work, huh?" Aunt Theresa teased Walt.

"Luggage and crutches don't mix," Walt laughed, then headed straight for the refrigerator for a snack.

"I'm sorry you didn't win, Hannah," Aunt Theresa said. "I talked to your uncle this morning. He phoned from Oklahoma when he stopped for breakfast."

"But I did win," Hannah said. "Most of all, the Lord won. I just went along for the ride." She grinned at Walt.

Walt rolled his eyes. But he was smiling.

Sam Sampson had left a low fire crackling in the lodge's big stone fireplace before going home for the night. Papa added some pine branches to the flames, and by the time he, Mama, and Hannah had dragged the rest of their suitcases inside, the fire blazed high.

Hannah placed her rose on the carved log mantle above the fire. "Scoot over, ol' hound," Hannah teased. She crowded into a big leather armchair, where Hunter dozed next to the open fire. "You've learned some bad manners since we've been away. You're expected to sleep on the rug. But for now..." Hannah pulled her flop-eared, tricolored hound across her lap to kiss his wet nose. "Did you miss me, sweetheart?"

"Ooo-woof!" Hunter laid his head in her lap, snuggling close.

Hannah's eyes fell on the heavy old dictionary on its stand by the window. Then she glanced at the rose Caylin had given her. Its petals had begun to droop during the plane flight home. "Come on, Hunter, get up. There's something we need to do."

Carefully, Hannah picked up her rose and the heavy book and brought them into the kitchen, Hunter padding behind her. She set the dictionary on the kitchen table with such a thud it rattled Walt's plate of apples and potato chips and homemade brownies.

"Homework already?" Walt asked, looking up from his book.

Hannah shook her head. "I'm going to press this rose," she said quietly. "I'll show it to Caylin after she and her parents get back from the Gulf of Mexico."

Hunter settled into his bed beside the kitchen stove.

"Good idea," Papa said. He slit open a piece of mail.

"Would you help me, Mama?" Hannah sat down

at the table. "I want this rose to remind me of what the Lord and I really won in Texas."

"Of course." Mama opened the big, antique dictionary. Near the back of the dictionary, Hannah knew, was a faded, pressed pink rose Hannah's grandmother had been given by a friend. That was so very long, long ago.

"Fetch the waxed paper from the drawer, please, Hannah," Mama said. "Two sheets the size of a dictionary page should be enough."

Hannah got the sheets of waxed paper and one of Aunt Theresa's brownies and sat down again. The warmth of the wood stove filled the kitchen. As Hannah watched Mama gently examine the rose, careful not to let a single yellow petal fall off, she felt tears slip from her eyes, warm on her cheeks.

"What's the matter?" Mama asked.

"Nothing's the *matter.*" It was hard for Hannah to put into words what she was thinking. Her tears weren't only sad tears or only happy tears. "I was just watching you all," she said, deciding that she would just have to talk and let the words come out. "I was thinking...thinking how I was such a creep and still no one was mean to me and everyone tried to help me and wanted to see me win. I don't know why you guys even liked me when all I cared about was myself."

"Big question," Mama said, looking at Hannah thoughtfully. "But the answer is pretty simple. We love you always."

"Even when I'm a creep?"

"Always."

Papa wrapped his hands around his coffee mug, warming them. "The Bible shows us how God wants us to be and live...and how to love people like Jesus did. We love you because of who you are, our daughter, not because of what you do. God loves *all* people because of who they are, not because of their performance. His love is unconditional, and He wants everyone to know Him."

Mama handed Hannah the rose. "Here, I'll let you put the rose in the book."

Hannah thought of her grandmother as she placed the rose on the waxed-paper-covered page of the dictionary. Mama helped Hannah cover the rose with the second sheet of waxed paper and carefully close the dictionary.

"This is getting to be a family tradition," Hannah said. "It kind of tells our story."

"It does," Mama agreed.

Hannah followed Mama's gaze out the front window, over the lake.

"You know, Hannah," Mama said after a moment, "there's a story in the Bible about another family long ago. The youngest son left his family and God, but his father loved him very much and never quit waiting for him to come home. When the boy finally did come home, lonely, hungry, and sorry he had left, his father ran to meet him."

"The story of the prodigal son?" Hannah asked.

Mama nodded. "The father received his son back into the family with open arms. God's like that—always waiting with open arms."

Hannah stared at the pages of the dictionary, not reading a single word, but seeing the whole story.

"It's God's story," Papa said. "Someday, when you have children, you can look at this rose and tell them the story of your family and another family long, long ago, and about a loving God."

Hannah sat still, feeling the warmth of the kitchen, letting the tears dry on her cheeks. *They're tears of wonder,* she decided.